Surviving with Joy

Receiving comfort from God while enduring trials from this world.

"You will show me the path of life; In Your presence is fullness of joy; At Your right hand are pleasures forevermore."

Psalms 16:11 (NKJV)

Shirley A. McBride

 www.trafford.com

North America & international
toll-free: 1 888 232 4444 (USA & Canada)
phone: 250 383 6864 ♦ fax: 812 355 4082

Dedication

Within the pages of this book very trying and very personal trials are shared for your spiritual growth. As these trials affected my entire family, I dedicate this book to my loving husband, Chris McBride. When tragedy struck our family, Chris first looked to our Father God for the very strength and peace He promises, and then extended that same love to Kristen and myself. Whereas, we are still a family today who enjoys an abundant life of Christ.

Additionally, I dedicate this book to my lovely daughter Kristen, who is truly a precious gift from God. Kristen is one stronghold that God uses on a daily basis to keep me strong and focused on Him. From Kristen I have gained strength which is indescribable. She is one of the reasons I wake each day ready to receive a new blessing from our Lord.

Appreciation

First and foremost, I thank my God and Savior Jesus Christ. For with Him (Them), these words would have never been written. God is the author of my life, and you will read in detail not only His presence in my life, but His very application.

Secondly, I thank my Pastor, Dr. Paul Noe. Not only did he allow God to use him during one of our trials, he has also supported our family above and beyond our expectations. Pastor Paul also helped with the editing of this writing and provided much needed advice and support.

Thirdly, my appreciation is extended to Dr. Keith Edwards, a retired missionary pastor, medical doctor, religious writer, and co-member of Sweetwater Baptist Church. However, to me he is a dear friend. Dr. Edwards also provided me with much needed godly direction through reviewing and editing this writing.

Forward

It is with great pleasure that I recommend to you the book, *Surviving with Joy*, by Shirley McBride. It is the beautiful testimony of how God has brought Shirley and her husband, Chris, through the loss of two precious children, Katherine and Faith. Her journey reveals how God's grace and strength have allowed her to *"Survive with Joy."* Her story will inspire and encourage those who are facing difficulties, coping with sorrows, and experiencing heartache. The McBride's have certainly demonstrated absolute faith and trust in the sovereignty, strength, and salvation of God in the midst of personal tragedy. In the pages of this book you will find hope, peace, and comfort when facing the storms and struggles of life.

A book is only as good as its author. I can assure you that Shirley McBride lives what she has written in *Surviving with Joy*. The McBride's are dedicated Christians, faithful church members, and hard workers. As their pastor, I have observed their commitment and devotion to Christ for years. It is genuine and real. Shirley's story is from a sincere and personal relationship with the Lord Jesus Christ.

May you be blessed as you read *Surviving with Joy!*

Serving Him Gladly,

Dr. Paul W. Noe, Pastor
Sweetwater Baptist Church
North Augusta, South Carolina

I first undertook to read Shirley's book with an editorial eye. I determined to look at vocabulary, verb tenses, subject and verb agreements and sentence structure. I glanced over that marvelous small guide to good English writing by Shrunk and White before starting to read this book.

Thus fortified by reviewing the book that most editors use to justify their corrections and criticisms, I began reading *Surviving With Joy*.

I soon found that the author's story of the loss of two beautiful children became so gripping that I could not maintain an editorial perspective. I would read several pages engrossed in the true story that Shirley was telling so vividly only to realize that I had not made a red mark anywhere. I would stop, go back, and try again to make suggestions to improve the text.

Shirley, and her husband Chris, are two of the finest Christians that I know. They have been challenged by having to walk through the valley of the shadow of death. While still young, and in the early years of their marriage, they had to see two beloved children die – one of a sudden, unexpected and unexplained illness.

In my years as a doctor, I have seen many people choose to be embittered by similar events. Yet Shirley and Chris maintained their trust in the Lord. Shirley relates in detail the loss of these children. Yet there is not a trace of bitterness. She does not blame the doctors or other medical personnel. She does not rale at fate nor lose her trust in God. She lives out the saying attributed to Charles Haddon Spurgeon that when you cannot trace God's hand you can still trust His heart.

I recommend this book to anyone who wants his or her Christian faith strengthened and especially to any who have suffered loss. Shirley's courageous walk through death's valley will encourage you.

Dr. Keith Edwards

Contents

Chapter 1

God's Guarantee

*"Fear thou not; **for I am with thee**: be not dismayed; **for I am thy God**: I will strengthen thee; yea, I will help thee; yea, I will uphold thee with the right hand of my righteousness." Isaiah 41:10 (KJV)*

Our Father God has made us many guarantees. In fact, A. L. Gill, Jr. wrote a small book entitled *God's Promises*, which contains 330 pages of His promises. These promises cover every aspect of our lives. God loves us so much that He promises to give us what we need, when we need it: *"Fear thou not; **for I am with thee**: be not dismayed; **for I am thy God**: I will strengthen thee; yea, I will help thee; yea, I will uphold thee with the right hand of my righteousness," Isaiah 41:10 (KJV)*.

God plainly assures us that He is with us and that He is our God. He does not state that He is only with us some of the time or that He is our God only for a short while. He is our Father God and is with us always—guaranteed.

Our Father is there when we sleep, wake, eat, cry, laugh, love, hurt, and so on. Furthermore, He promises to be there giving us the strength and help we need even before we ask. He upholds us in righteousness when we are too proud or too week to stand on our own.

I have suffered many circumstances in this world when God carried me through valleys—many valleys even before I was living whole-heartedly for Him. I can not, however, tell you of a time when God was not right there holding me, filling me full of His promised strength, help, love, and joy even in the midst of difficult circumstances.

In December 1991 my father noticed a lump in the left side of his chest. Within a few weeks, he was diagnosed with malignant melanoma. Melanoma is the deadliest form of skin cancer. A person's chance of survival is lessened with a diagnosis of internal cancer rather than topical (effecting only the outer layer of skin). My father's was internal. The cancer had grown inward to the middle of his body from a mole on his back.

When the doctors removed this tumor and described it as looking like an octopus—a round ball with legs stretching out from all sides. One of the legs had reached the lymph glands under his left arm indicating that these abnormal cells were now spreading and traveling throughout his body. Right away treatment was given to stop this infestation and my father received positive reports each time he met with his doctor.

About one year after his diagnosis, my father began experiencing severe pain in his lower right abdominal area. I can remember him stooped over, holding his side as tightly as possible, with a look of desperation on his face that I had never seen before. What troubled me most was the knowledge that my father could handle pain better than anyone I had ever seen before. But, this pain was different. Dad was almost crippled.

He struggled trying to do the things he loved. He and I even went hunting one morning, as we did often. I knew that he did not feel well, but he absolutely loved the sport so I gladly went with him. It was not long after we were settled in our stands, waiting for that opportune moment of taking a deer, that I heard dad walking back. He stopped by my stand to let me know that he just could not bear the pain that morning to hunt and that I should stay while he went home. I could not though. I was afraid for him and concerned.

That very week he was diagnosed with over seven melanoma tumors in his liver. The doctor told my parents that whoever named that particular organ, named it right, because we cannot live without our liver. Right then everyone knew dad was now terminal.

Just as God promises in *Isaiah 41:10*, *"I will strengthen thee, I will help thee,"* He did. Dad was sent almost immediately to Duke University to receive an experimental drug treatment. No one knew or could expect the outcome as the drug had not been tested long enough to know of any effects of either long- or short-term.

Receiving this drug once a month over a nine-month period, my father once again entered complete remission. Every tumor that had grown in his liver had vanished completely. Dad was back to himself, his health seemingly better than ever—life was great, thanks to just one of God's guarantees: *"I will uphold thee with the right hand of my righteousness."*

A few months later, mom and I noticed dad doing and saying "strange" things. Once while he and I were driving home from work, he pointed quickly through the window and said, "Look at that deer!" There was no deer. At first I thought I just missed seeing it until he did it again the next day and several days after. Another time we were eating dinner and dad was earnestly looking for something all around his plate. Puzzled, mom and I looked at each other. I then asked dad, "What are you looking for?" He answered, "My cake." The cake was in his left hand.

Mom and I did not have to discuss this situation. I think we understood and just did not want to say it out loud.

With his next diagnosis, the cancer was in his brain. There were three tumors, one on each side of his brain and another on the back. Surgery was not an option as the tumors had grown so rapidly that by the time one was removed and he had healed enough for another surgery, the other two would have over taken his brain completely. This time there were no treatments for cure, no experimental drugs, and no hope given by the doctor. Mom was told that further treatment would be primarily for comfort. Dad survived only a few months beyond that diagnosis and entered his eternal life on July 19, 1994, at 10:15 p.m.

Everyone living in this world has two assured possessions: a birth date and a death date. Both of which are decided by God—*"Your eyes saw my substance, being yet unformed. And in Your book they all were written, the days fashioned for me, when as yet there were none of them,"* *Psalm 139:16 (NKJV).* God looked upon us before we were, He looks upon us each day, and He'll look upon us in eternity—**if we choose Him in this life.**

After my father received eternal life, God carried me for months. Dad was my best friend. I trusted him more than anyone; even God at that time. Once the grief weakened and the sorrow passed, I concentrated on living. I had been engaged for a couple of years and had not been able to marry because my fiancé Chris was working his way through college and I had been helping mom with dad. But, everything had changed. Chris graduated college, dad entered his eternal home, and we made our plans.

Chris and I married on February 18, 1995. I could not remember ever being happier. We simply enjoyed life and each other for a couple of years. Then **that** urge hit. My motherly chemistry was pressing forward. It was time to have a baby and start a family.

Chris and I discussed having children and prayed asking God for guidance and assistance. We knew we would need God's assistance as I had been told by three doctors that I could never conceive. A fourth doctor stated that I could conceive, but not on our own. We would need fertility drugs and possibly other scientific methods of conception. We prayed and left everything to God.

We came to a decision of trying to conceive in December 1996. My luck not being the best, I experienced a ruptured cyst on my left ovary that very month. I was taken to the hospital in dire pain, bent over, and unable to stand straight. After several tests, I was told that an ovarian cyst had ruptured and I would need to stay off my feet for a few days and follow-up with my gynecologist the next week.

As I was in my doctor's office discussing the matter, I mentioned to her that we were ready to try and have a baby. My doctor's eyes quickly enlarged as she told me "no!" She said that I would have to wait another month as some women have these ovarian cysts monthly and that I would miscarry should one rupture while pregnant. Her advice was to wait another month and if there was no cyst, then I could stop the birth control and begin trying. She also said for us to not get our hopes up. With the endometriosis that I had for so long, I would not get pregnant right away and that after six months of trying with no luck, she would then begin a regimen of fertility drugs.

Chris and I were not upset at all. We were not in a hurry to get pregnant and had even discussed that getting pregnant closer to or even mid-summer might be better for us. Ultimately, we were leaving this to God and His timing.

God demonstrates in His Word that He has a planned time for everything in our lives for He knows what is best for us, as well as what is best for His plans with this world. Two of the many examples of his timing are found in *Genesis 17:9-22* and again in *Luke 1:5-20*.

First of all in Genesis, Abraham and Sarah had grown very old in age, well past child bearing years, when God Himself approached Abraham and told him that Sarah would have his child. To which Abraham and Sarah actually laughed in disbelief since Abraham was 100 years old and Sarah was 90. These two knew they were well past the age of conception and found the idea, even though coming straight from God, humorous. These two knew their bodily limits, but they did not understand God's limitlessness. In verse 22, it is written that they would be blessed with a child "at a set time". In Genesis 21, it is explained that God visited Sarah, as He said He would, and Sarah conceived and bore Abraham his son Isaac *"at the set time of which God had spoken to Abraham."*

Then at another time in history the book of Luke tells of Zacharias and Elizabeth waiting until late in life to be blessed with a child "in its own time." Again, God had a plan. This baby was John the Baptist who paved the way for Jesus.

Children are a great gift from God (*Psalm 127:3*), of which He has a purpose. Therefore for God's purpose to be fulfilled, we have to "wait" for His timing in all things.

We followed my doctor's orders and waited out the month and there was no cyst! I immediately stopped the birth control pills and we went on with our plans in February 1997.

Just two weeks later while at work, I experienced a wave of sickness through my stomach. I instantly wanted to throw-up and thought that I would right on my desk. I hurried to the rest room and stood there waiting to be sick. Nothing happened. My first thoughts were, "Oh no—not a stomach virus." But and hour later there were still no ill feelings. I kept thinking, "What could that have been?"

About thirty minutes before work ended, I thought to myself, "No way, I could not be pregnant this fast!" The excitement was building and I could not wait for Chris to pick me up from work so that I could tell him the good news and get to the drug store for a pregnancy test.

On the way home I told him of my experience and asked him to stop by the drug store. I wanted to know right away. But Chris was pessimistic. He told me not to get my hopes up and reminded me of what the doctor said about the endometriosis and that we could try a while before ever getting pregnant on our own. But, he took me by the store and we then went straight home.

I went immediately into the bath room, completed the test and waited those long three minutes for the results to show. To my very surprise was that beautiful, pink, vertical line—POSITIVE!

I ran to tell Chris only to watch him fall immediately into a bewildered state. He said, "We've only been trying for two weeks!"

I said, "Welcome to fatherhood!"

We were both so happy and excited. The joy gleamed from our eyes, we stood with heads high and shoulders back. The only other times I can remember being this happy and joyful was the night Chris proposed and our wedding day.

We chose not to tell anyone until our news could be confirmed. It was during this time that we got news that one of my uncles had fallen ill. He was diabetic with failing kidneys. My mother wanted to see him, so Chris and I drove her to Bristol, Tennessee, where he was hospitalized.

Once there, mom seemed to be a little more at ease. Uncle Bill looked in better health than we expected to find him. There was a moment leaving the hospital that mom and I were alone and I just could not hold the secret anymore. I told her that I was pregnant; unofficially of course. Although she was delighted with the news, mom soon became concerned. She said, "You came on this trip." "You should not have traveled so far in your condition." I assured her that it was too early in the pregnancy to worry about all that and that everything would be fine.

We enjoyed the rest of our trip, visiting with our family and then returning to our homes. We got back to work and confirmed our secret with the doctor. It was time to tell!

I of course called mom to confirm that I was pregnant and to let her know that she could tell my brothers. We then went over to Chris's parents and told them. I have never seen anyone become so excited so fast. This was their first grandchild and they both were elated.

I could not wait to share my news at church the next Sunday. But, I was too late. Chris's mom had called everyone she knew. By the time I got to church, everyone was telling me my good news.

Over the next few weeks life could not have been better. I was certainly on "cloud nine". I always wanted a family of my own and had prayed for that many times as a teenager (even before I was a Christian). Now God was answering those prayers in His time.

God hears everyone's prayers (Consider *Psalm 4:3; 5:3; 6:9; 55:17; and 65:2)*, and it does not matter if you have not yet accepted Christ into your heart. If a person is going to pray (talk) to God, then that person believes there is a God (or at least thinks there might be). Even with the smallest amount of belief, that person then has faith. A person must first have faith in order to accept Christ. Many times people pray first and when God moves in their life, they then have evidence of God's existence. Their faith then strengthens, along with their knowledge, which brings them to a point of asking Christ into their heart and in control of their life.

One Saturday afternoon as I visited our bathroom, my joy quickly turned to fear. There was the slightest color of pink on the paper. My heart dropped. I quickly checked again with new paper, and there was more pink—it was blood!

I quickly got to the phone and called my doctor's office. The doctor on call instructed me to get off my feet, he called in a prescription of antibiotics, and told me to call my doctor back on Monday morning for a check-up. He did reassure me that a little spotting was not unusual for some ladies and for me not to become alarmed.

By Monday, however, my doctor gave me different news. As she checked me, she said that I had a great deal of blood inside. Again I was reassured to not worry. She sent me home to be off my feet completely until further notice.

I followed her instructions, but my situation worsened. Each day seemed to bring more and more bleeding. I reached a point of being uncomfortable in certain positions and finally my doctor explained to both of us that I was bleeding so heavily that I was sure to miscarry. She went into great detail explaining the pain I would feel as the miscarriage began and instructed me to get to the hospital with the first of any abdominal pain. She even explained that we would need to perform an abortion if the bleeding increased at all in order to save **my** life.

As I stood in her office listening to her instructions, I became upset. At this point in my life, I was too shy a person to speak my thoughts or desires to anyone except Chris. I did not want anyone to perform an abortion while my baby still had a heartbeat no matter what! But I could not bring myself to voice this to my doctor.

Chris and I left her office crushed! We got into our car, shut the doors, and I quickly, emotionally expressed my feelings to Chris. I explained to him that I did not want an abortion if our baby was still alive under any circumstances. He reminded me that the doctor said that I could loose my life. I told Chris that I had lived my life and that I would not take our baby's life and that I was okay with whatever God chooses—to take one or both our lives, but the choice was His and not ours.

The next few weeks brought the same prayer opportunities. The bleeding kept it's same pace, I was on bed-rest, and our biological and church families prayed daily. They supported us with meals and companionship; helping in the only way they could.

At about the twelfth week of pregnancy, the bleeding stopped! I could not believe it and neither could Chris. I had finally reached a point of grace. As written in *1 Timothy 1:14, "And the grace of our Lord was exceedingly abundant, with faith and love which are in Jesus Christ." (NKJV)* We got to the doctor's office and the baby's heart beat was strong and clear. Everyone was excited. The doctor ordered a sonogram so that we could finally see our baby for the first time.

The sonographer was so excited to be performing this procedure for us that it emanated all over her body. As she began the scan she had the monitor turned so that we could see our baby immediately. And there it was. A beautiful small form of a body, with the loveliest heartbeat ever heard.

Our excitement quickly subsided, however, as we were not ready for the next picture. As we watched while she scanned different views, another sac appeared on the screen. This one did not have a small body form nor did it have a heart beat.

I had to ask, "Is that another sac?" and she said quietly, "Yes." We immediately became solemn. The sonographer did not say another word. She just turned the monitor away from our sight, typed a lot, and printed out a few images. She told me that I could now get dressed and have a seat in the waiting room, and then she went to see the doctor.

As we found ourselves back in her office, we also found our doctor explaining that there is no way to be sure that there was ever a baby in that sac since only one heartbeat was ever recorded.

Chris and I know in our hearts that there was another baby in that sac and that baby right then was in heaven with our Father and will be in heaven waiting for us when we arrive.

Our feelings were mixed. We were elated to still be pregnant, but at the same time saddened to be separated from our other child, whom we would not see, embrace, or experience until we reach heaven.

From that point forward, our pregnancy was routine. We learned in the next month that we were having a girl, and we began preparing for her birth; buying a crib, some clothes, and all the beautiful, pink necessities.

I can remember being the happiest I had ever been. I was getting the right mix of chemicals throughout my body. Even when Chris would say or do annoying things that would upset me, I just did not care anymore. Nothing bothered me or got to me the way it had before pregnancy. I loved being pregnant and could see the excitement of fatherhood growing in Chris daily.

About seven months into the pregnancy, our baby started to change things a little. She found my sciatic nerve and camped out on it until she was born. I will remember that stinging, stabbing pain forever. Due to that pain and an elevated blood pressure, my doctor immediately put me back on bed rest. My pain was so severe at times that I had to get up and pace. It was the only way I got any relief, although never enough.

Finally, I had reached the thirty-eighth week of pregnancy. I had endured that pain for two and a half months. As I was seeing my doctor on a usual weekly check-up, she told us something we did not want to hear: "Your baby is showing signs of distress." She feared that the umbilical cord was wrapped around her neck so she decided to perform an emergency C-section[1] right then.

The next thing I knew I was in an operating room strapped down with both arms straight out and numb from the waist down, with Chris at my right side. As the doctor began to perform this operation (where the patient is wide awake), she adjusted the stainless steel light

---

[1] Caesarian Section – a surgical incision through the abdominal wall and uterus performed to deliver a baby.

over my bed which made an almost perfect mirror. I could see her every move.

I watched closely as she made the outer incision and began to work on the uterus. I wanted to see my baby born. Chris noticed that I was staring straight up and thought that I was in shock or that something else had gone wrong. That caught the anesthetist's attention which made him check me for problems. When they realized that I was just watching the show, they shook their heads in disbelief, and left me alone. Although it was not long before my doctor readjusted the light and my show was over.

A few minutes later Faith Ashley McBride was born on October 28, 1997. Our beautiful little 5-pound 15-ounce package straight from God had arrived at 5:25 p.m.

It was a time of celebration. Both our families filled the hospital that day: my mother, all four of my brothers, their families, along with Chris's parents and both of his brothers.

Life could not have been better. I absolutely loved motherhood, and Chris had instantly become a perfect, loving father. Faith was truly loved from the moment of conception and I did not realize just how much more I could love someone until I looked at her beautiful face as Chris held her to me in the operating room. When she was laid in my arms a while later, the love I felt for her was indescribable. I can only imagine the love God has for us when we are reborn into His family. He gives us children as the greatest gifts of all. In *Psalms 127:3 (NKJV)*, God says, *"Behold children are a heritage from the Lord, the fruit of the womb is a reward."*

Take a moment and try to imagine the love God has for us when we grow to our age of accountability and we choose Him. God is not one to chase after us. He is waiting for us to realize His love for us and to run to Him so that He can experience a real love from us. In return, we receive **ALL** of His guarantees of love, joy, peace, patience, kindness, goodness, faithfulness, gentleness, and self-control (*Galatians 5:22-23*). Along with these guarantees, we also receive strength (*Habakkuk 3:19*), power (*Romans 1:16*), and companionship (*Matthew 1:23*).

Ecclesiastes 7:1(NKJV) says *"A good name is better than precious ointment; and the day of death than the day of one's birth."* We must die to ourselves (stop our worldly ways) and choose God as our Father and accept His son Jesus into our hearts. We as humans are not capable of loving like the Father who is always there for us, always forgiving, always caring, always leading, and always giving. We only have to love Him as much as we are humanly capable, and ask Him into our hearts and lives in order to receive the abundance of love that He readily guaranteed us through Jesus. *"For God so loved the world, that he gave his only begotten Son, that whosoever believeth in him should not perish, but have everlasting life," John 3:16 (KJV).*

Chapter 2

My Walk With Our Father

*"Behold, the virgin shall be with child, and bear a Son, and they shall call His name Immanuel," which is translated, "**God with us.**" Matthew 1:23(NKJV)*

Trial One

Throughout the next year Chris and I truly enjoyed Faith while learning to be parents. I was a mother who enjoyed the hassle of dealing with the carriage in public and looking for changing rooms. It did not take long to develop a list of restaurants which had the baby changing stations and to avoid the ones without.

Both Chris and I enjoyed taking Faith to visit our parents. Faith was the first grandchild on his side of the family and his parents' joy in Faith overflowed from head to toe every time we walked through their door. Grandma could not take her into her arms fast enough, and Papa could barely wait for Grandma to pass her to him. I will never forget how their eyes widened and their faces lit-up with excitement each time they held Faith.

As for my mother, she could not have too many grandchildren. When I would step through the door, mom was there with hands and arms out-stretched for Faith. Mom would take her straight to a rocking chair, wrap her blanket a little tighter and send me off to sit and rest. Then she would rock and love her granddaughter for hours.

After a few months, Chris and I discussed having more children. We did not want Faith to grow up an only child. We both had brothers and understood that the love siblings have for one another is unmatched by any friend you gain. But, we also wanted to wait about four years and space them out a bit.

It is funny though, how we try to make plans with lives that belong to our Father God, especially when His do not match ours.

When Faith turned one year old, I was able to wean her from breast feedings and return to the use of birth control. We were married for two years and discontinued birth control to get pregnant with Faith so we were sure that we could control when our next baby would arrive to some degree.

But to our surprise, when Faith turned 15 months old we found ourselves pregnant again. That is what we get for not asking God about His plans. Even funnier was the way God let me find out that I was pregnant.

The three months back on birth control, I found myself having more aches and cramps than before and in different places. I had convinced myself and Chris that I was dealing with some sort of ovarian cyst problem that caused more pain and irritability so I went to see my doctor.

As I sat in her office explaining my **chronic** aches and pains and feelings of sluggishness and irritability, she quickly assured me that I did not have an ovarian cyst of any sort, but that I had **chronic** PMS[2]! As she said those words, I thought: "You are wrong. I am not just PMSing, I have a real problem."

So I asked, "Well, what can I do about this?" "Is there treatment for it?"

She said, "Yes, there is treatment and it's with the use of a different birth control." Oh, what a relief. At first I thought I was going to have to take another drug the rest of my menstrual life.

My doctor began giving me instructions on waiting until I finish the course of birth control that I was currently on in order to begin this new pill. But as she was talking, I realized that I had just finished my course the Sunday before, it is now Friday, and I should have started my cycle last Wednesday. With the use of birth control my cycle was like clockwork. I always took my last pill on a Sunday and began my cycle on a Wednesday.

When she finished her instructions to me, I then told her that I should be menstruating at that very moment and was not. Being a very cautious person, I told her that I would take a pregnancy test before

---

[2]   Pre-menstrual Syndrome

starting this new pill—just in case. She jokingly replied, "Well we can help with that problem too, just let me know."

I thought to myself, I cannot be pregnant again. We were not planning to have another baby this soon.

On the way home, I could not get to a pharmacy quick enough. Afterward, I stopped to pick-up Faith from a sitter, and went straight home to let Chris know what was going on.

After we talked I passed Faith off to him and darted off to the bathroom to take the test. Again, waiting those three minutes seemed like eternity, but watching that beautiful, pink line appear before my eyes was breathtaking. You guessed it – **POSITIVE** again.

I could not wait to tell Chris and I was filled with so much joy that I could only laugh and smile with this great news. Chris said, "You gotta be kidding, we were gonna wait a few years." So I had to ask, "Are you happy about this baby." He said, "Oh yes, it's just sobering."

So I called my doctor's office right back and told them the good news. To which they replied, "You need to be confirmed," and made me an appointment for the next week. Chris and I already knew in our hearts that we were expecting again, but we chose not to tell anyone until we the doctor's had their confirmation.

That next week we were sharing our news with our family and friends. Our parents were ecstatic once more. Our friends were happy and could not believe that we were having our children so close together. Everyone got a little laugh when they realized we were not planning to have another baby so soon. As for Chris and me, we were happy to receive another precious gift from God.

For the next four months, life was great. Being pregnant again had me back on "cloud nine" where I felt great all the time and nothing could bring me down. For me to be pregnant was close to being in heaven, where I know everything is perfect.

Chris went along with me to our fourth month check-up so that he could be there to see the first sonogram and learn of the baby's sex. We really enjoyed the sonograms. It was like getting another gift soon after the receiving the gift of pregnancy.

As the sonographer scanned through my abdomen to see this small miracle growing and living inside me, she quickly pointed out the heart beat and took all the necessary measurements. Then she got very quiet.

I noticed that she kept scanning the same areas over and over. She had already turned the monitor from our view and typed more than I had ever noticed before while expecting Faith. I asked was everything alright, and she said yes, that she was trying to learn of the baby's sex. She said that the umbilical cord was placed right between the legs and that she could not get the baby to move in a way that would help her view.

Finally, she said that she was not going to be able to tell us the sex as she could not get the cord out of her view. She asked me to get dressed and wait for the doctor to see us. Right then I felt something was wrong, because we never before had met with the doctor after a sonogram.

I was a little more concerned because my doctor was out on maternity leave herself. We were waiting to talk with another doctor within the practice.

Eventually the nurse came to direct us to the doctor's office. However, the story was written on her face. I had never seen anyone with such a saddened, scared look on their face. She never said anything to us, she just walked us to his office and left quickly.

When this doctor came in, he began telling us that something was seen on the sonogram that brought them a little concern. He indicated that there seemed to be a neucleofold at the baby's neck, which might mean Down Syndrome and that the baby's heartbeat was not as regular as it needed to be. He quickly reassured us that these might be problems, but to be sure we needed to see a specialist to have these findings confirmed or denied.

The next morning we were in the specialist's office. I was too trusting in people and still did not feel an urgency about this visit. I felt like we would have another sonogram with better equipment and be told that we have a perfectly healthy baby and go home as happy as we had arrived.

In this office, however, the doctor was right with the sonographer as the exam took place. They did not turn the monitor to our area of view and made sure that they used words we could not understand.

Finally the exam was over, and the doctor turned to us and spoke words that I will never forget. He said, "Your baby has Down Syndrome, severe heart disease, and hydrocephalus." He continued to explain that Down Syndrome meant retardation and that we would not know the full extent until birth and that the baby's face would be sagging as this is where the term 'Down' is derived. As for the heart disease, he could only tell us that our baby had a severe condition. We would need to see a pediatric cardiologist for final diagnosis, but he could already tell that the heart was not pumping blood correctly. His explanation of the hydrocephalus was a condition having too much fluid on the brain and that the baby's head would be enlarged and the severity of retardation would be increased. But even though this is a serious condition, it was the least of the baby's problems and would be addressed last.

He went on to insist on performing an amniocentesis where a large needle is placed through the abdomen and into the uterus to collect fluid. This fluid, he said, would let them know the extent of the baby's disorders.

Being in complete shock and crying profusely, we agreed to the procedure, which was performed almost immediately. We were told that the results would take a week to arrive, and we were then sent home.

I have never in my life cried so much, so long, and so uncontrollably. We stopped by our cousin's house to get Faith and I could not even speak. I could not bring myself to say the words that would explain our baby's condition. Chris did the talking, and I did the crying.

When we finally got home, I was completely broken, still in shock, still crying uncontrollably. Faith knowing something was wrong, but not knowing what, had quietly fallen asleep on the way home.

I found myself sobbing on the couch alone. Chris is someone who needs to be alone with God during difficult times. So he had left me and gone outside for a long walk through the woods. I knew that he was also broken and that this is when he probably cried while taking his hurt and concern to our Father God.

Even though I knew what Chris was doing, I felt abandoned. I was sobbing and crying out to God asking why and begging Him to heal our baby. As much as I tried to stop crying, I cried even harder. With Chris walking out the way he did, I felt that I was going to have to handle this situation by myself. As I laid on the couch, I looked to God and poured out my soul. I told Him that I could not care for this baby or Faith the way I was crying. I told Him that I could not stop crying as I had tried several times, and the tears and whaling would just not stop. I remember saying out loud to God, "You're gonna have to stop these tears so that I can care for my children!" Not yelling at God, just deeply in distress.

As soon as those words passed from my body, the tears stopped. God filled me with strength and assurance just as He promised in *John 14:18, "I will not leave you comfortless: I will come to you." (KJV)* I could not understand the way I was feeling and how I could not cry anymore. I just knew that God had immediately answered my prayer. He had come to me. He had wrapped His arms around me and provided all the strength and comfort that I needed.

I then collected myself, dried my face, and made those awful, dreadful phone calls to our parents. I asked them to call our brothers and let them know, because I just did not want to continue repeating our situation.

That evening, I called my Sunday school teacher and gave her the details. I asked if she would share our prayer concerns with the class. I told her that I was not going to attend the next Sunday because I did not want to see the sorrow in everyone's eyes.

But then, she asked me something that once again jolted me into reality. She asked, "What's wrong, you're too calm?"

I told her that I had cried out to God and had pleaded with Him to take away the tears and replace my strength and how He had responded instantly. This statement was new for me. I had not been one who witnessed for God openly. I always did in my heart, but was always too shy to ever respond openly.

Afterward I called my three best friends. These were Christian friends whose prayers I desperately needed and wanted. As I shared with them our baby's health concerns, each one cried and did not say much at all. They only mentioned that they were sorry for us and would pray. I finished each call feeling a sense of comfort, knowing that my friends would be praying.

The next couple of months were as routine as possible, with a lot of added doctor's visits. Each month I met with my Obstetrician, a specialist, and a pediatric cardiologist.

My doctor and specialist had many times told me that I should "consider my options," along with their explanations of how this baby was too sick to survive. They said that my body would spontaneously abort between the sixth and seventh months of pregnancy.

My doctor had even explained the pain and bleeding I would endure at the time of this abortion, and that I should really consider my options to abort now rather than wait for that experience.

I finally reached my boiling point! Once she explained her feelings and professional opinion on my circumstance, God filled me with strength again. I explained to her first and foremost that I was a Christian. I trusted and believed in God. I told her that I absolutely would not consider and abortion as life and death situations were not for me to decide. I explained that my baby was a gift from God and that if He chose to end her life that would be okay with me, but I could not.

I reached the seventh month of pregnancy, and had not miscarried and was experiencing no signs of miscarrying. I decided to quit a part-time job and remove unnecessary stress in my life in order to give our baby a real chance of being born alive and at full-term.

I'll never know if removing that stress helped or not, but our baby Katherine Hope was born alive and as well as she could be on September 1, 1999, at the same 38 weeks gestation as Faith had been born.

God was truly in control of her birth. Katherine was delivered by a scheduled C-section because the specialist feared that the stress of natural birth would have stopped her heart. Because of her heart condition, the operating room stood full of about 25 medical professionals ready to jump into action to revive her when she did not breathe on her own.

That is when I realized just how serious her condition was. I began to be a little nervous myself. But, I kept thinking, God is in control and whatever happens will be His will, for He knows best, and is in control as He wrote in *Psalm 31:24, "Be of good courage and He shall strengthen your heart, all ye that hope in the LORD." (KJV)*

As the specialist performed the C-section and delivered Katherine, God showed-off His power. Katherine did not need any of the extra professionals in the room. Not only did she breathe on her own, but she cried louder than Faith did at birth. Chris was even allowed to carry her to the Neonatal Intensive Care Unit (NICU), with a stop by the waiting room to proudly show Katherine. The only medical device attached to her small body was a thermometer.

When Katherine was just 24 hours old, she endured her first heart catheterization[3]. The cardiologist then discovered that she had her very on venous system, which made a 15-20 minutes procedure turn into an hour procedure. For instance, the typical artery he used in everyone from the groin to the heart was not the same for Katherine. Her artery led from the groin to over the right shoulder and down into the back. The doctor had to map-out her venous system to find the way to her heart. Once again, God was displaying His power in that when we are not even put together right, He can make us work.

Well at seven days old, Katherine had her first open heart surgery. Her little heart, just the size of our thumb, needed a lot of repairs, but at this point the doctor was only correcting a hole in her aorta. If this had been left undone, she would have died within a matter of weeks. She sailed right through this surgery with strength and healing. She came off the life support with no trouble at all and we were now looking forward to taking her home soon.

Chris and I just kept learning new things about Katherine each day. Now that the surgery was behind us, we were faced with getting Katherine to take a bottle on her own. During her first weeks of life she was tube fed with a line that was inserted through a nostril and down her throat and into her stomach. The time had arrived for Katherine to have her first bottle at three weeks old.

As Chris and I sat together in a not-so-private intensive care unit, I cradled Katherine in my arms and offered her a bottle. Not only did she not know what to do with it, we learned very quickly that many babies with Down syndrome are not able to swallow.

I am pretty sure that the nurse knew right away that Katherine's swallowing mechanism just was not working. But, she kept encouraging us not to give up. She would say things like, "You have to give her time to figure out what to do with the nipple," and "She may think this is some kind of game, but she'll get it in a minute." Brokenhearted, we soon realized that she just could not suck and swallow and that she would remain on tube feedings for a while.

Finally, we were told that Katherine would be ready to go home the next week. In preparation, Chris and I had to take a few classes. We

---

[3] Inserting a catheter into a vein and manipulating it to reach the heart for an internal examination.

learned to administer the many medications she would always take, CPR, (Cardiopulmonary Resuscitation) and tube feeding before taking her home.

Take just a moment and think about what most moms and dads learn when taking home their newborn of only a couple of days: breast or bottle feeding, holding their head with the right amount of support, wrapping them in warm or cool enough clothing, changing diapers, and so on.

Chris and I took our baby home a month after birth and we literally had to become specialized nurses to watch for her skin turning blue to indicate heart problems; knowing CPR in case she stopped breathing due to her heart condition; and how to insert a tube through our baby's nose, down her throat, and into her stomach, just so she could be fed and receive medications to keep her alive.

As we were leaving the hospital, one of the escorting nurses asked if I had any other children. When I responded "Yes, a 23 month old," she gasped and quickly looked at the other nurse with very fearful eyes. She then asked if I had a lot of help. She explained that Katherine would be a full-time job, and followed-up by saying that she would not take a baby home in Katherine's condition with another toddler to care for.

That was the moment that I realized just how sick Katherine was. From the moment God stopped my tears when I was pregnant and filled me with extra strength, I had not been nervous and upset through this whole time—until now.

As we walked on to the parking area for us to leave, I did not say another word. I kept telling myself that God was in control, and that the ICU nurse had given me her number, and had assured me that I could bring Katherine right back to the ICU if I needed help with anything.

We, the proud parents, were taking our baby home for the first time at four weeks old. We stopped at Chris's grandparent's home on the way as his grandmother was housebound. We knew that we would not be taking Katherine out for a while and we really wanted them to see her.

Great Grandma McBride could not believe that we brought that bundle of answered prayer and joy for her to hold and love. I had never seen Grandma McBride look so happy and excited. It did not even bother her that Katherine had the feeding tube inserted and taped to her face.

The next few months were strenuous and tiring, but we found them quite enjoyable as Katherine strived each day. We were told that she would not gain weight as other children, because of her heart disease. With the Down syndrome she would have low muscle tone and just lie without being able to move and play. However, Katherine did not know that, and just like healthy children, she gained right on schedule. She was reaching for toys, and learning to sit up by six months of age. (*"He sent His word and healed them, And delivered them from their destructions,"* Psalm 107:20, NKJV).

Katherine Hope

Katherine was truly a joy even though each month was riddled with doctor's appointments. She visited the cardiologist, physical therapist, and pediatrician each month. She received treatment from physical therapists twice weekly in our home. Even though this was a rather rigid schedule, it was worth every minute to see Katherine become excited and her face glow with happiness. She would grin from ear to ear as if she would explode with joy. All my time with her reminded me of God's grace and His **guarantee**, *"God with us" (Matthew 1:23b, KJV)*.

I can remember several times Faith would say, "Look at her mama, she sure is happy." Then I would remind Faith that we sure were fortunate to have a God who would take care of our every need and give us so much joy through such an unfortunate circumstance.

We had to live like hermits because Katherine could have been found in severe danger had she contracted the simplest of colds. So we did not go many places at all. We would only venture to the doctor's offices out of necessity and then visit our parents only after making sure no one had been sick recently. Katherine was never taken shopping, or to any fun places, in order to protect her from common colds and viruses, which could have proven fatal had she contracted either. Since her heart was malformed, and her lungs and body were weakened, the most insignificant cold would have been life threatening to her. Therefore, our lives consisted of home and doctor's offices, with an occasional visit to our parents.

Just a week before Katherine turned seven months old; we made our usual visit to the cardiologist for a routine check-up. As we worked through the process of getting blood pressure readings, which had to be taken from all four extremities, and having blood drawn, I was not prepared for what the doctor said as soon as he stepped into the examination room and took one look at her from the doorway, "She's ready for the next stage of heart surgery, and we have to do it in the morning." I was thoughtless (not to mention speechless).

I could not believe what he was saying. Katherine was doing so well, thriving in most all areas. "It could not be time for the open heart surgery," I thought.

After collecting my thoughts, I asked him why she needed the surgery so urgently as to schedule it for the next morning. He replied that she was turning blue. She was not getting enough oxygen and was really dying before our eyes at a rather slow rate.

With Katherine's particular heart disease, her heart was not connected to the lungs correctly. While she was a small infant, her lungs could handle the flow of blood and provide her body with the right amount of oxygen. But, with her striving so well and gaining weight normally, she had reached the point where her lungs could no longer provide the necessary oxygen to her body.

Amazingly, Chris and I could not see her turning blue. One would think a condition like that would be highly noticeable to parents, but seeing her daily and the cyanosis developing gradually, Katherine looked normal to us.

That next morning we found ourselves in the Children's Medical Center of the Medical College of Georgia. I had taken Faith to my mother during Katherine's hospitalization since we were not sure how long we would be at the hospital.

I was allowed to carry Katherine all the way to the operating table in order to be with her right up to the point that the anesthesia was administered and she was asleep for the procedure. Katherine was especially playful that morning. She would smile real big and reach for my face. I can still feel her tiny hand on my cheek today and see that huge smile as I walked her to the operating room.

I also remember how her happiness turned to fear as I laid her on the table. She starred at me desperately with her big, blue eyes as the anesthesia mask was being placed over her mouth and nose. I was so glad to have been there with her all the way, and I am sure she received comfort from looking into my eyes and not into the eyes of a stranger.

The next few hours were spent with family, our preacher, and a few friends in the waiting room. A nurse from the operating room would call every hour to give an update. Although each update received was good news, it seemed days between each call.

Finally our doctor emerged and told us that Katherine sailed through this surgery with no problems, and that she was doing fine.

Not long after, Chris and I joined Katherine in the Pediatric Intensive Care Unit (PICU), where we found her back on life support and completely lifeless. Our doctor explained that the life support was giving her body a time to heal and accept the changes with less stress. He assured us that after a few days they would remove the tubes, and she would breathe on her own.

The next morning, I found myself sitting there alone with Katherine. Chris had missed so much work that he had to go back so we would not loose our insurance. Our cardiologist had left for a much needed vacation the day after her surgery and would be gone for a week. That left me a little uneasy since we had not seen any other doctor with Katherine during all seven months of her life. But, I understood his need for a vacation of rest and relaxation.

As I sat there that morning—praying, wondering, concerned, happy that she was doing well—in walked the surgeon for a check-up. He was an older, quiet man, and I am sure he had no personality what-so-ever. We had met with him on several occasions before Katherine's procedures, and he was always the same—unappealing. But, he was described as the best pediatric surgeon in the United States, and that is what we wanted for Katherine—The Best!

As he walked in the room—no good mornings, no eye contact, no facial expression—he went straight to Katherine and looked at her incision and vital signs, all the while his hands were clasped behind his back, he suddenly stopped moving and uttered the words, "You have to have pristine lungs for this procedure." Then he turned and walked away.

For a moment I could not breathe. My first thought was, "There is nothing pristine about Katherine—she has Down syndrome." That is when I first understood the indescribable peace I felt about bringing her in for this procedure.

From the moment I learned of Katherine's condition while still pregnant with her, I had not felt peace. I was worried, concerned, and heart broken that she was not healthy and would have to endure so many surgeries and therapies just to become somewhat healthy. But, when her doctor said that we would have to do this surgery just two days before, a peace flowed over me that I could not describe. The only thing I knew for sure was that God was in complete control.

God was preparing to bring her home and heal her in His wonderful way. I knew that Katherine would not survive this hospitalization. As much as it hurt to understand this, and as much strength as it took to fight back the tears, I had peace within.

The next few days were uneventful. Each day I saw a different cardiologist; each having their personal opinion about her condition. I quickly reached a point where I would not even ask questions. I would watch them arrive in the morning, hear them contradict the doctor from the morning before, watch them write their opinion in her chart, and then watch them walk away.

They had become so accustomed to working with the terminally sick that they had lost their compassion for the concerned, love-struck, scared-stiff parents anxiously waiting to hear any good news. Most of the time, I was ignored as though I was not even in the same room.

Then the day of change came. Katherine developed a high fever; and, after several blood tests, the doctors discovered that she had a staph infection. These are not words anyone ever wants to hear. This is an infection caused by a germ on the equipment used in the hospital. Staph infections are so severe that very healthy adults have been known to die from them.

Her infection had developed in the lungs; therefore, believed to come from the breathing tubes which were a part of her life-support system. No matter what antibiotic the doctors prescribed, nothing was working. Her fever climbed higher as her body grew weaker. That evening our worst fears began coming true. Her heart began to slow.

The crash cart was summonsed, the room filled with doctors, nurses, and respiratory therapists—all trying to keep her tiny, burdened heart from stopping. I can remember her pulse lowering to the teens and thinking, "She's going home."

As the nurses and therapists performed CPR, the doctor at one point had both hands on the sides of her head as if she just could not think of anything else to do. She was constantly repeating, "Come on Katherine", "Come on Katherine", "Come on Katherine," when suddenly her heart slowly regained strength. Her pulse slowly climbed back to normal, the fever left, and she stabilized.

We all began to breathe again. The doctor even gave God the credit. She admitted that she had done all she could and did not know what to do next. Feeling a huge sigh of relief and continually thanking God in my thoughts, I was drained. I had never felt the way I did at that very moment. To be right on the edge of feeling that part of your world was completely crashing one minute and the very next minute everything is fine. That is a very hard transition to make in 60 seconds.

Katherine was stable for the next 24 hours. Nothing eventful took place. Katherine's tiny body had been bloated from the saline used to keep her heart from stopping the night before. Now as she lay lifeless, her eyes could not even close completely. She was very pale and looked as though she were dead. It was very hard to look at her. The only way of knowing she was still alive was seeing her vitals on the monitor.

The next morning, yet another unknown cardiologist had a turn to 'check-in' on Katherine. One look at this lady and you knew she was serious. She did at least say good morning when she entered the room, and as she looked over Katherine, I could not help but notice the look on her face—of anger.

I walked over to the opposite side of Katherine's bed and asked this doctor what she thought of her condition. Looking over the top edge of her reading glasses, and staring straight into my eyes, she replied, "Your baby is not going to make it." She continued to explain why, but my thoughts shut down at that point, and I did not hear any of her explanation. I could only look at my beautiful daughter, laying there so lifeless and thinking, "What a trooper." With her frail, messed-up system, along with her low-toned muscles, she was surely fighting the good fight. I tuned back into what the doctor was saying and heard, "Katherine probably would not live through the night."

As there was nothing more to say, the doctor completed her survey of Katherine's condition and left within a few minutes. I could not take my eyes off Katherine. I felt desperate, wanting to do something and could not. I leaned over to her and told her just how much I loved her. I told her what a good baby she had been with striving through her ailments and enduring all her check-ups and therapies, and still having the strength to smile at me after each, as if to say, "I love you, mom." I told her that it would be okay for her to leave and find her place in Heaven. I told her how much God loves her and wanted her to be with Him so that she can be completely healed. . . I told her good-bye.

Then I called Chris and told him that things were worsening, and that he should come to the hospital. When he arrived, we had lunch together and afterward I explained Katherine's condition as stated by the doctor. Chris would not accept it. He said, "No, Katherine is not gonna to die, we're gonna take her home in a few days." I then tried to tell him how I felt God telling me before the surgery that we would not taker her home. Chris would not accept that either. He just said that I was talking out of fear.

As we joined Katherine after lunch, God's plan began to unveil itself. The doctors were becoming agitated about her blood work. They began administering more antibiotics and checking her vitals more often. Finally, we were told that another staph infection had infiltrated her system—this time her heart.

This ICU lead physician explained that her body was tired, and because this infection had attacked her heart, Katherine was going to have a tougher fight on her hands. Immediately, we knew that her condition was serious and grave.

All afternoon and into the evening blood was taken, antibiotics were administered, and prayers were spoken. At about 9:45 p.m. the doctor wanted to meet with Chris and me. We knew that there would be no good news. He explained the situation of the staph infection and her weak system. Before he could complete the meeting, Katherine took a turn for the worse. Her heart slowed drastically.

The doctor yelled, "Crash Cart!" Immediately her room filled with nurses, doctors, and respiratory therapists all working to revive this tiny, little, worn-out soldier who had fought for so long. The doctor would yell orders and the nurses and therapists were yelling responses and taking turns performing CPR.

All the while Chris and I stood watching believing, and not believing, the scene before us. Although I could not bring myself to say it, I was thinking, "What are you doing?!" "God's calling her home."

After a short while, the doctor threw his hands in the air with frustration of having nothing else to try. I could see his mind working, searching for anything to save Katherine. Then our eyes met from across the room and for a moment we just looked at each other. Finally I nodded my head ever so slightly—yes. From that he stopped everyone's effort. He pronounced her dead at 10:15 p.m. on April 7, 2000.

The nurses quickly began preparing her body, securing the tubes and removing the IVs. As I stood trying to grasp the reality of what had just happened, I thought of my father and how peaceful he looked when he died, and I wanted to see Katherine. I walked to her side, with the nurses still preparing her for us to hold, and there was that peace. Her tiny body was still and calm.

I know that God allowed my father, and now my baby, to have a peaceful expression on their face to fill me with the peace of knowing that they were alive and well with Him at the very moment their life ended on earth. (*"We are confident, I say, and willing rather to be absent from the body, and to be present with the Lord,"* 2 Corinthians 5:8, KJV).

Chris and I could not stop the tears that fell as we held our baby for the last time. Knowing that we would never again see her smile and play in our home, and that we were going to miss her desperately for the rest of our lives, the grief covered our souls.

I saw a positive change in Chris that night. An event took place in his life for which he was not prepared. At first, I believe it was shock, and afterward I believe he realized just how precious life and family are. Over the following months and years we grew closer than I could have ever imagined, and our relationship was certainly stronger than ever. We enjoyed our family placing our concentration on raising Faith to love the Lord.

Trial Two

As my love for our Father God grew into a beautiful love affair, I learned that He often uses unexpected ways to speak to His children. I truly believe that He also exercises His sense of humor in this way.

When Faith was four years old, just two years after Katherine entered her mansion in heaven, she came to me one day while I was preparing supper, and with her hands on her hips, looking me straight in the eyes, she asked, "Mama, are you gonna have another baby or what?"

I am sure you can imagine my surprise as I stood speechless for a moment. I answered her with, "Well, your father and I haven't discussed having another baby so I'll have to get back to you." I told her that in the mean time she should pray about what God would have us do.

Chris and I had not mentioned that possibility at all since Katherine joined Christ in heaven. I was not sure what he would think about Faith's thoughts on the subject. I was not really sure of my thoughts on the subject. Later that night I shared Faith's question with Chris and asked his thoughts. He simply said that he was not sure. So we committed the idea to prayer and did not mention it for a while.

God had a plan, though. In February 2002, I was pregnant again. I was excited about the baby and to see God work in my life again, but quickly realized my excitement was not shared by family and friends.

Shock overcame our family as we shared our news with them. One of my brothers asked, "What are you thinking?!" While my mother-in-law let me know that I could tell everyone this good news and she told only a few.

When our church family learned of our pregnancy, we were met more with "are you sure about this" than "congratulations." I was shocked. These God-fearing family and friends did not believe God could produce a healthy baby through Chris and me after Katherine. My response to them was "God is in control" and if He chooses to bless us with another unhealthy baby then He will also bless us with the strength to take care of this one just as He had with Katherine.

On October 21, 2002, Kristen Ann was born, very healthy and very beautiful. Faith was extremely excited as she had received her answered prayer. She did not want a little brother, and she was quite adamant about her decision. Life was good and God is certainly great.

Our next few years were wonderful. We enjoyed our family, going to church and taking vacations. Everything we did was modest as Chris earned our only income. We did not mind because I enjoyed caring for my children, and I knew that God preferred moms and dads caring for their children themselves. Furthermore, God provided everything we needed. There were years that I did not believe we would be able to take a vacation, but we always did through God's provision. (*"But my God shall supply all your needs according to His riches in glory by Christ Jesus," Philippians 4:19, KJV*).

Early in 2005 rumors began where Chris worked that their budget was going to be reduced significantly, and that layoffs would surely ensue. Chris and I responded as usual and took this concern to God in prayer. We did not ask for his position to be spared the cut, but for God's will to be done in the matter.

By the first of July, God's will surfaced. Chris received noticed that his position, among others, had been terminated. After 15 years of full time service, his position was no longer needed. He was given a notice of 90 days, during which he did not have to report to work, and would still receive his normal pay. Instead, he and the others could use this time to job search. Chris took advantage of this opportunity and spent more time at home. He also took handy-man jobs along the way and sent out resumes and waited upon our Lord to answer.

God even sent an opportunity through the handy-man work for a job at Edisto Beach. Chris was able to take all of us and we were allowed to stay in the house being renovated and enjoy the beach for a full week. This was an opportunity that we had never received before, and we truly had one of the best times of our lives.

Faith and I would rise early to go out shell searching right after dawn. We would get back just in time to have breakfast with Chris and Kristen, and then go back to the beach for swimming and playing while Chris worked. We would go back for lunch and a nap, wait for Chris to reach a stopping point in his work, and then we would go back to the beach and enjoy the afternoon together. As if that were not enough, when we would get back from the beach about dark or shortly after, Chris and Faith would shower off the salt water and climb right into the hot tub. We lived it up like we had never done before. All through that week, we praised God for we knew that only He could provide this type of reward during such an uncertain time.

Although there were a few bites of interest to hire Chris from several companies, nothing panned out fully during the 90 day period. He reported into work his last week of the notice period to finalize the termination process. God went with him. While there, Chris was approached by a co-worker who told him that there was a job opening where her husband worked. Chris followed through on this opportunity and was hired the next week.

Wow! Is God ever awesome? He knew we were alright, and knew just when to open the next door of opportunity before our manna from heaven in the form of a paycheck ran out.

During this time God had also brought me an opportunity as a ministry assistant supporting two ministers at a local church. This position was truly perfect for me as I love the Lord with all my heart.

Again, He had worked out everything. A dear friend of mine volunteered to provide childcare to Kristen while Faith was in school. Then my mother-in-law would pick them up at the end of school and keep them with her until I got home around 5:30.

Everything seemed perfect until Kristen started having separation anxiety. I was having a difficult time dropping her at the sitters because she would just cry and scream all the way there and beg me not to leave her. My Heart was being torn.

I knew that God had provided this job since He opened all the doors and worked out every minor detail. I had even denied the position at one point, just to call back and let them know that I was interested two weeks later.

I became very distraught over this job, and my absence was affecting Kristen. I was sure Faith was being affected too, but she was seven and understood more than Kristen. Faith also enjoyed having Grandma pick her up at school. But one day, I could no longer hide my feelings at work. One of the ministers I supported called me into his office and discussed this with me. I explained the situation and then was surprised at what he told me in response.

He said, "I knew all along that you were going to take this position, even when you turned it down. But, God told me that when you got here you would not be here long." He went on to explain that he saw me in a role of leading a women's ministry at some church.

My surprise at his comments came from the fact that God had also told me that I would not be there long, and that he had a reason for sending me to that Church. However, I did not know the reason or how long I would be there.

Over the next few weeks Kristen was just not adjusting to my absence and neither was I. Finally, I resigned the position and agreed to work part-time through the first of the year to help them through the holidays.

I still did not know why God sent me there. Then one day I was approached by one of the ministers I supported. He was desperately looking for a speaker for one of his singles groups. Someone had canceled, and he did not have anyone to fill in. As we discussed this, I felt the Holy Spirit nudge me to volunteer. I did, and he accepted a bit reluctantly. I now knew why God sent me to this church. I could surely share about Katherine and the CMC Ministry, which was a ministry He called me to start through my home church, Sweetwater Baptist of North Augusta, SC.

This ministry provides food closets at MCG for the parents of hospitalized children who cannot afford to purchase meals during their child's stay. God also grew this ministry to allow for closets in the pediatric clinics to provide snacks to children receiving life-saving treatments. Additionally, I would be able to share about God's control and presence in everything I had experienced.

When the night approached, however, I prayed and asked God to take control of my words and speak through me. I asked Him to supply the testimony that He wanted and not what I thought needed to be heard.

He took that prayer and ran with it! God had me stand before these 20-25 single adults and discuss my suicidal, depressed teenage years, and how He had carried me through all that even when I was not a "child of God". To my disbelief, I was sharing a part of my life that I had ever only shared with my husband. When the night was over, I received such a relief from bondage. God knew that I did not want to share that with anyone, but I had to in order to be complete in Him and to allow Him to be completely in control of my life. God instructs us in *Proverbs 3:5-6, "Trust in the LORD with all your heart, And lean not on your own understanding; In all your ways acknowledge Him, And He shall direct your paths." (NKJV)*

I did not understand why God was having me share such a personal and private experience with complete strangers. I can tell you that He gave me the strength to share this past circumstance, and I was certain that He had a reason. When I had concluded this testimony, joy raced through my very being.

The next week I overheard that minister discussing the fact that one of the young men there that night was suicidal. He had been ministering to him all weekend. I knew right away why God had me share that particular testimony; he was using me to talk to only one of those 25 or so in attendance. I may never know if my words had any sort of affect on that young man, but I know that God was in control of the situation, and that His word does not return void to Him; *"So shall My word be that goes forth from My mouth; It shall not return to Me void, But it shall accomplish what I please, And it shall prosper in the thing for which I sent it," Isaiah 55:11, NKJV).*

From that point on, I really lost my zeal for the ministry assistant position. I knew that I had fulfilled God's desire for me there. It was time for me to return fully to my family. However, I was honoring my word and planned to work through the end of the year, which was only about six weeks.

A couple of weeks later, I was comfortable. I thought that I knew God's plan for me, and I had just experienced a summer of watching Him work miracles in our lives. We were making plans for worshiping Christ through celebrating His birthday—Christmas. There was excitement in the air.

However, on the night of December 6, our life took a turn that we just were not expecting. About 10 p.m., Faith called from her bedroom, "Mom, my stomach hurts!" Faith had been diagnosed with an elongated colon a few years earlier and because of that condition she suffered severe pain as a result of constipation from time-to-time.

At first, I thought she was having another bout with constipation. I brought Faith and Kristen to my bed for the night to allow Chris to sleep in their bed for an undisturbed night's rest. A while after coming to my bed, Faith's stomach pain worsened. She was crying out quite a bit, just as she had done all the other times. This time, however, she began vomiting, her stomach pain would stop for a while, and the cycle would begin again. Additionally, she had a low-grade fever. I was convinced that she had a stomach virus.

All through the night, we were up and down with the stomach aches and vomiting with neither of us getting much sleep. Faith vomited throughout the day Wednesday, and the stomach pains weakened to varying cramps. Faith did not eat much because she did not have an appetite. I considered this another symptom of a virus.

By Thursday things had changed. Faith felt well enough to get out of bed, eat crackers, and sip on Gatorade® and Coke®. I just knew she was nearing the end of this virus, so we kept the course of nibbling and resting to allow the virus time to pass.

Her dad would come in at night and spend time talking to her and making plans for the weekend; to go pick-out our Christmas tree and decorate for the Holidays. Her time with Chris was always special to them both, as they were the best of friends. We could tell, though, that she still was not feeling her best because she mostly just listened and nodded her head "yes" to his questions and comments.

As Friday morning began, Faith vomited once again. This surprised me because she had not vomited for quite some time. When I got her cleaned up again and back into bed, she immediately told me that she was hungry. I told her that was what I had been waiting to hear because that meant she was getting better. I also told her that we did not want to push things and that she needed to keep on eating crackers and drinking small sips of Coke® for a while longer.

Chris went in to see her before leaving for work. He told her how much better she looked, and that if she kept getting better they would go out early Saturday and pick out that Christmas tree.

As she ate and drank, she moved into the living room with Kristen and me. The three of us sat and watched a movie together. When it was over I asked if she wanted me to start decorating the inside of the house for Christmas, or if she wanted to wait until next week when she would feel like helping me. She told me in the sweetest voice, "Yea, you go ahead now and do it."

I was hoping that by decorating, she would start feeling the excitement of the season and would begin feeling better. However, Faith crawled onto the couch and stretched out across the pillows and quickly fell asleep. I remember thinking how odd that was for her to fall asleep so fast, but remembered that she had been up so much the past few days that she was simply tired and needed sleep. I got my shoes on to go outside and get the decorations from our shed; and, as I started walking through the kitchen, Faith sat up on the couch and called, "Mama." I looked back at her just in time to see her eyes rolling back into her head and her body relaxing into the couch. By then I was by her side holding on to her as she started vomiting from her mouth and nose all at once.

My first thought was, she cannot breathe like this, so I held her head so that the vomit would drain and she would not choke. Then there was no movement. Faith was limp in my arms, I began screaming "no" over and over, and then the words turned to "she's not breathing" over and over. I was terrified and in shock. The only thoughts I had were God telling me, "She's with Me now."

I could not bring myself to let go of Faith physically, and I screamed for Kristen to bring me the telephone. I dialed 911 and frantically told them what had just happened, and that she was not breathing. I was so frantic that the dispatch lady told me that I was going to have to calm down so that she could understand what I was saying. She then began talking me through CPR as she sent EMT's[4] to my home. I was so grateful that she was talking me through CPR because even though I had taken the course many times and had to learn the procedure before bringing Katherine home from the hospital, my mind was not comprehending what my eyes were seeing, and I could not function.

Even with the 911 operator telling me what I needed to do, Satan was attacking through my thoughts. My mind kept telling me, "I can't perform CPR on my child," while Jesus had control of my body and was already going through the motions. How desperately I wanted the EMT's to arrive, take over, and help Faith breathe again.

I kept talking with God in my thoughts, wondering why I had to be alone. Why could not Chris be here helping me or doing the CPR? To make matters worse, I did not even have time to call Chris, nor did I know how to get in touch with him at his new job.

Finally, I could hear the sirens, the EMT's were here! The problem now was letting them in. To unlock and open the door meant I had to leave Faith. I really did not want that. Quickly realizing I had no choice, I ran to open the door. My legs were so weak I felt I would fall with each step I took. I remember thinking they felt like noodles, and I could not understand how I was standing on them. *("And he said unto me, My grace is sufficient for thee: for my strength is made perfect in weakness," 2 Corinthians 12:9; KJV).*

I threw open the door and called for them. A technician ran in behind me and straight to Faith. I was shocked as he just knelt beside her and looked at the vomit on the couch and floor.

My thoughts were, "What are you waiting for, get to work!"

Another technician ran in and knelt on the other side of Faith, he quickly assessed the situation, and the first gentleman said, "Let's do this!"

---

4 Emergency Medical Technician

They then began CPR and defibrillation[5] in efforts to regain her heart beat. I stood holding Kristen and watching them repeating the defibrillator many times. Faith's body vigorously pulsed with each shock wave. My heart pulsed with anticipation with each shock wave— to no avail. They then moved her to a gurney, strapped her down, and proceeded to transport her to the hospital.

I grabbed my purse and we followed them out the door. As I looked out past the technicians I could not believe who I saw standing in my yard. There was my Pastor, Dr. Paul Noe, and our Youth minister, Daniel Brady. All I could think was, "Who told you?" I never spoke those words, but I was truly relieved to see a familiar face and to be able to place Kristen in someone's care so that she would not have to watch any more of the events unfolding. Pastor Paul gladly took Kristen to my Mother-in-law Audrey McBride, and then he met me at the hospital later. (*"Who comforteth us in all our tribulation, that we may be able to comfort them which are in any trouble, by the comfort wherewith we ourselves are comforted of God," 2 Corinthians 1:4; KJV*).

When we arrived at the Medical College of Georgia, I jumped out of the ambulance, ran to the front of the truck, still amazed at how I was standing on my weak legs, and waited urgently for them to bring Faith into the emergency room.

As we traveled through the halls and into a room, I felt as though I would fall to my knees at every step. Finally, she was in a room with two doctors and many nurses and respiratory therapists working diligently to regain her heart beat. There I stood, completely alone, in the hall. No sight familiar. No face ordinary. I wanted desperately to do something, to be with Faith, to know what was happening.

I looked up when I noticed someone walking toward me. A deputy sheriff approached, with a pen in one hand and a notebook in the other. He looked me in the eyes and said, "What is her name?" I answered Faith McBride. He wrote her name in his book and turned and walked away.

A few moments later, a lady approached me and began to pray. She told me her name, and that she was one of the hospital's chaplains. She held me tight and never stopped calling out to God.

---

[5] A machine used to stop the fibrillation of a heart.

Just a minute or so later, a nurse told me that a family member was there, and asked my permission to allow him back to where we were. I could not imagine who had gotten there so quickly. I told her that any and all family could come back. With God's grace my Father-in-Law, Billy McBride, rounded the corner. He immediately asked about Faith, and when I told him she was not breathing his next words were prayer.

Many times in my Christian life I've prayed, "Not my will, but yours Father", meaning those words whole heartedly. But as Billy ended his prayer with those exact words, everything inside me screamed no, not this time! My Father God had already told me that Faith was with Him back at home. I knew with all my heart that she had already been escorted to her mansion in the sky by Jesus Himself (*John 14:2-3*), only it had not been confirmed by the doctors.

A nurse from Faith's room came out and asked if I wanted to be with Faith and I told her yes, but did not want to get in the way. She assured me that I would not be in the way, and walked me into her room and right to her bed side. There I stood at Faith's feet holding on to every ounce of hope that I had left, while the chaplain was holding on to me and together we prayed without ceasing (*"Pray without ceasing," 1 Thessalonians 5:17, NKJV*).

Within her room was a flurry of activity; each person knowing exactly what to do. As each one worked to regain Faith's breathing, only the doctors would make eye contact with me. The two doctors working together would yell out procedures, and the nurses and respiratory therapists would leap into action. Finally words came that I wanted to hear, "We have rhythm!"

Oh how I thanked God desperately only to have Satan crush my hope with another person yelling out, "It's only the meds," meaning that the medication given to Faith was the only thing making one part of her heart beat again.

Then one of the doctors approached me saying that they had already gone above and beyond their normal procedures for anyone brought in to the hospital in this condition, and that nothing they had done was working. She then told me that they were not giving up, but wanted me to know our exact situation.

I recognized this doctor. She was the same Cardiologist who was with us the night Katherine almost died. She was the one who gave credit to God when Katherine survived that night.

She then asked where Faith's father was. I explained that he was at work, a fairly new job, and that I did not know of a way to directly get into touch with him. I told her that I had family members working on getting him there. She immediately turned to a nurse and instructed her to send a deputy Sheriff to where he worked.

Here I stood in a room full of strangers working to regain the life of my first born daughter who had just turned eight years old in October. I had never known fear and pain at the level I was experiencing both at that very moment. Still on weakened legs, I could barely stand, feeling like any minute I would fall to the floor, and afraid that if I did, I would no get up. It was a true relief to have the Chaplain put her arms around me and pray with me as I could feel God's power holding me upright through her.

Inevitably the other doctor approached me, and again I was being told that they had already done more to save her than is usually performed. He went on to explain that she was not responding to anything, and that I had to give them permission to stop their efforts, otherwise she would be placed on life support, although her life was already gone.

I could not believe what I was hearing. How could Faith have been getting better earlier that morning and now just a couple of hours later, I'm standing here giving them permission to pronounce another one of my daughter's dead.

Faith Ashley

I shook my head "yes" and while every part of me went numb. The doctor told them to stop and for someone to "call it" and another person yelled out, "Dead at 12:15 p.m. on December 9, 2005."

My body froze as I screamed, "No!" over and over. My legs went completely numb, my knees locked, and I could only stand there motionless, screaming no and crying profusely. The doctor quickly grabbed me and held me on one side as the Chaplain held me from the other side.

I absolutely could not move, could not breathe, as my world exploded around me. They quickly sat me in a chair and called in my family members and pastor who were all there. With all of us crying and in complete shock, my thoughts now were with Chris. Where was he, who was with him, and when would he get here.

Moments later, Chris walked into the room and seeing Faith lifeless on the table, he collapsed to the floor. Before I could move to get to him, several people were helping him up. He just cried out, "no" and "why" and "what happened" over and over. To which no one had an answer.

A short while later, Chris and I were alone with Faith. I was a little surprised when his first question was, "Shirley, what time did they pronounce her gone?"

I told him 12:15, but could not bring myself to ask why. I just sat there looking at Faith, and then at Chris, and back at Faith. He then explained that as he was driving over the Savannah River, just minutes from the hospital, God told him that he needed to get strong because Faith was now with Him. Chris said that he argued with God saying that she could not be, she was so much better this morning when he had left for work. To which God replied, "She's with Me now, you need to get strong."

We were not saying much to each other. We sat starring at Faith and I am sure both wondering why and how this could have happened. I kept searching in my thoughts, wondering what I had missed while caring for Faith those last few days. Absolutely nothing came to mind.

After what seemed to be hours, the charge nurse came in and told us that someone was there to speak to us. She said that we would have to wait for the coroner to come to the hospital to inspect Faith's body, to speak to us, and that we would take him to our home for inspection.

A criminal investigator walked in. She walked right to us and looked me straight in the eyes and asked me what happened. After I explained the details of those past few days, she asked me to write that explanation on a piece of paper, as she handed it to me. She then went on to explain that Faith's body would have to undergo an autopsy and asked if I had any objections. I told her no and that I needed Faith to have an autopsy so that I would know what just happened.

This investigator walked away, and there we sat alone with Faith again as I wrote the explanation. Writing the words that explained those events was the hardest thing I had ever done. Seeing those words in print made what I had just experienced real. This was not just a horrible nightmare that I would wake from. I would not regain a sense of security after realizing I was just dreaming. No, life had just delivered an incredible blow.

I quickly became angry. Satan was still there attempting to knock me down further. I was insulted that an investigator had questioned me. Although this process is standard for all children who are dead on arrival at an emergency room, I knew that Satan was using this method to put me on trial in his world. Having to wait on the coroner was another of his tricks. We were forced to stay at the hospital in the same room where Faith had been pronounced dead, and where her deceased body still lay. Once the coroner arrived, I would yet again be put on trial and suspected of foul play.

Our Father God delivered me from that trial when at about 5:30 p.m. another nurse came in to tell us we could leave. She explained that the coroner had been called to an accident and it would be much later before he could inspect Faith's body. From this I knew that God had over come Satan. For us to be able to leave without further inspection, and to be told that the coroner would not be coming to our home after all, I knew that the investigator saw and heard what she needed to cast blame away from me. Thus God was there and controlling the circumstances in His favor, and holding Satan in his loosing place. (*"So when this corruptible shall have put on incorruption, and this mortal shall have put on immortality, then shall be brought to pass the saying that is written, Death is swallowed up in victory. O death, where is thy sting? O grave, where is thy victory? The sting of death is sin; and the strength of sin is the law. But thanks be to God, which giveth us the victory through our Lord Jesus Christ,"* 1 Corinthians 15:54-57, KJV).

Before leaving I asked a nurse where to find their rest room. I had been at the hospital for about six hours now and I really needed to relieve myself. However, I was amazed when she pointed down the hall and told me to take the first left and the rest room was the second door to the left. Again I found myself walking alone, still on weakened legs, not sure if I would make it to the rest room without falling to my knees.

I remember thinking, "I can't believe they're letting me go alone – my child just died." But, I reached the rest room, relieved myself, and stood at the sink washing my hands. As I looked up and saw myself in the mirror, I did not recognize the person looking back. That person was completely broken, had disheveled hair, no make-up, completely pale and in deep despair.

Instead, I saw Satan starring back at me laughing. I could hear him say to me, "Where is your God now?" and "Look at what I was able to do."

To which I starred right back at him and said, "Satan, if you didn't like me before, you're surely not going to like me now!"

I assured him that I would work harder and do more for God my Father who loves me completely. I let him know without doubt that I would not turn from God under any circumstances.

I then turned to walk away and immediately noticed that the strength had been restored to my legs. I no longer felt as though I would fall to my knees—I felt as though I could run. I knew that at that moment God had restored my strength as He was proud of me choosing Him over Satan. (*"Therefore, my beloved brethren, be ye stedfast, unmoveable, always abounding in the work of the Lord, forasmuch as ye know that your labour is not in vain in the Lord,"* 1 Corinthians 15:58, KJV).

I joined Chris and we walked together through the waiting room to leave. There were still many of our dearest friends waiting to personally share our pain. Each of them accepted us with open arms, tear stained faces, and hearts of love that could only come from God.

We then left for home. We had to stop by Chris's parent's to get Kristen, where again there were many, many people expressing their love and concern for our family. I could only concentrate on Kristen and the task of telling her that Faith will not be with us anymore, as she had gone to heaven.

We walked in and I went straight to Kristen, took her in my arms and holding her as tightly as I could, I carried her to a back bedroom and sat on the bed and told her that Faith had died, and that she was now living with God in heaven, and that she would not come back to our house ever.

Surprisingly, she never said a word. As I spoke to her, she just looked at me with the saddest, blue eyes and frowning face that I had ever seen her wear. Then we just sat there holding each other, clinging so tightly that I did not think we would ever let go—and I did not want to.

Shortly after, Chris walked in and sat with us. I told him that I really needed to go home. I just wanted to be with my family, and I knew that Chris needed an explanation of the events that had taken place.

Everyone tried to get us to stay there, and I finally told Chris's cousin, that I really needed to clean up where Faith had vomited on our couch and carpet. She emphatically begged to let her go and clean for us. But I explained that some things a mother just had to do herself, and for me that was one of those things.

Once the three of us got home, I walked Chris through the events that had taken place that morning. It became clear to Chris that Faith had entered eternity there in our home as the substance left on the couch and carpet was bile.

I gathered a pan and brush and prepared myself to clean. Afterward, Chris and I did not have much to say. There was nothing left to discuss, and we simply held each other and cried as the realization became clear and the shock began wearing off.

Just minutes later, people started arriving. As they entered, faces expressionless, minds blank, they would just utter the words "I'm so sorry" and then hug us with the strength of lions. Some sat and held our hands and prayed while others would come in and say, "I couldn't stay away, I don't know what to say, so I'm just gonna sit here and hold your hand."

They sat on the very couch where our beloved, first-born daughter Faith met our Lord and Savior Jesus just hours earlier.

Once everyone left, we tried to take Kristen to bed. It was at this time when realization set-in with her. After I dressed her for the night, she looked up at me and said, "Where's Faith Mommy, I can't sleep without Faith."

My heart broke all over again. I explained again to Kristen that Faith was now living in heaven and will never come to live with us again, and she exploded into a whaling cry screaming, "no, no, no, no!"

Chris and I both just grabbed her and held her as tightly as we could. There was nothing else to say, and we all cried together until she fell asleep in our arms.

So there we were in bed, in the dark, enduring the most horrific torture of our lives. Only Kristen was sleeping. Chris and I cried out, "God help me!" over and over. Many times Chris said that he wanted to just get a gun and kill himself because he could not handle the pain. I tried talking to him and reasoning with him. Through the tears I said, "You can't do that Chris. Kristen and I are still here and we desperately need you."

I went on to remind him that we had to live for Kristen. It was our job to lead her to Christ, just as we had done Faith. I lay there all night completely and totally broken. My entire being experiencing brokenness and pain like never before. At times, I could not even breathe and could not stop crying. But on top of the pain I was feeling, fear had set in. I had never seen Chris so low and broken. I had never heard him suggest even a hint of suicide.

I was afraid that if my fatigue won and I fell asleep, Chris might get up, get a gun, and join Faith. So I lay there being tortured with every possible emotion and feeling known to man listening to Chris wail cries of desperation and rock back and forth endlessly.

Finally God allowed the morning sun to rise. Chris and I got up and walked back into the living room, where all I could see were the events of the day before replaying horribly in my mind. I collapsed to the floor where Faith's body last laid and cried furiously. Chris fell to his knees and held me tighter than ever before, begging me to get up. I can remember him just saying my name over and over and over, "Shirley, Shirley, Shirley!"

My strength was gone. I could not move or speak. I could only cry uncontrollably as the realization set-in. My body fallen to the floor in a heap, my fingers wrenching the carpet where Faith last laid, and begging God, "Why?!" (*"Likewise the Spirit also helpeth our infirmities: for we know not what we should pray for as we ought: but the Spirit itself maketh intercession for us with groanings which cannot be uttered," Romans 8:26, KJV*).

Chapter 3

Receiving God's Offerings: Leaning On God

*"For we have not an high priest which cannot be touched with the feeling of our infirmities; but was in all points tempted like as we are, yet without sin. **Let us therefore come boldly unto the throne of grace, that we may obtain mercy, and find grace to help in time of need.**" Hebrews 4:15-16, KJV.*

My strength was gone. This was the second time in four years that I not only said farewell to a daughter, but I had to give the doctors permission to pronounce them dead. Shock had complete control of my body. I could not sleep or eat, and sometimes not even breathe. There was one thing I did have—strength.

God was now standing for me as I stood for Him in that ER bathroom and chose Jesus over Satan. I knew that my strength came from God's love for me, one of His many children, and I truly believe that the abundance of strength I now have came from a God who is pleased and proud of His child's (His servant's) decision. (*"The LORD is good, a strong hold in the day of trouble; and he knoweth them that trust in him,"* Nahum 1:7, KJV).

The days that followed were agonizing. Having to go through the motions of making arrangements for Faith's funeral, receiving family and friends wearing faces contorted with sorrow and fear to the point that most of them were speechless, and then walking into that funeral home for the first time and seeing Faith laid to rest in a casket.

As I thought of having to do each one, my very being shouted "no!" I did not want to do any of those. But as our dear brothers and sisters in Christ began knocking on our door and entering with the tightest, warmest embraces, once again God was providing just what was needed.

In *Hebrews 4:16* God says, *"Let us therefore come boldly unto the throne of grace, that we may obtain mercy, and find grace to help in time of need." (KJV)* Our Christian brothers and sisters were boldly bringing the throne of grace to us. Each one of them first had to allow God to strengthen them so that they could greet us in our place of sorrow and brokenness. Each one of them, not knowing the words to say, came in with grieving eyes, partial smiles, and each one uttered something like, "I love you," "I'm here for you," "I'm praying for you," and most importantly they would say, "I'm sorry." Each one shared our pain in the only way they could.

Astonishingly, with the first person through the door, peace engulfed me. With just their presence, God was giving me an assurance that He was still there. (*"Peace I leave with you, my peace I give unto you: not as the world giveth, give I unto you. Let not your heart be troubled, neither let it be afraid," John 14:27, KJV*).

The worst thing our family and friends could have done would have been to stay away. Had they not come to us, our despair would have multiplied a million times over, leaving us in the very bottom of grief's pit.

As each one came, whether they spoke or not, we were told, "I love you and I'm here for you!" Therefore we would not and did not have to endure this pain alone.

Knowing that our friends and family had the strength to be with us personally assured me that they had the strength to pray for us as well. God heard their prayers and answered with strength in an indescribable abundance. (*"Let us therefore come boldly unto the throne of grace, that we may obtain mercy, and find grace to help in time of need," Hebrews 4:16, KJV*).

As mid-morning arrived, so did the autopsy results. Chris's father came in with a very solemn look on his face, sat down at our table, and asked how we were. Next he told us that he had received the autopsy results and began to explain that Faith died from a very rare condition known as "mal-rotation of the colon." This birth defect was the very reason we had taken her to the hospital several times with severe stomach cramps since she was four years old.

I could not grasp what I was hearing, I yelled 'no' and collapsed on the couch in the very spot where Faith met Jesus, uncontrollably crying and screaming 'no' and 'why' over and over again.

This news simply could not be true. Faith's stomach condition had been thoroughly tested and diagnosed as an elongated colon. The doctors explained that she would eventually grow into her colon and her constipation and cramps would end. I could not believe that she had now died as a result of her stomach condition.

My mother, Mary Mabe, and oldest brother Bo came in just at that time. I was so glad to see Mom and we instantly embraced each other and cried with all our might. All I could say to her was, "Faith was going to die anyway."

After collecting myself, Chris and I were able to tell them the autopsy results, and to explain that the stomach virus had most likely triggered the binding of the mal-rotated colon, which then stopped the blood flow to her intestine and eventually caused the toxic shock that took Faith's life.

I could not fall apart with my mother there. She had always been a pillar of strength. I can not remember ever seeing her out of control, but she cried the hardest I had ever known when she walked into my home.

My brothers have always told me that I was just like our mother. One might say that she had taught me to be strong over the years as I watched her endure and survive many circumstances. Knowing that God is always in control, I know that God used her influence over my life to help prepare me for my trials.

We must realize that even though God can provide us everything needed by Himself alone (*Isaiah 40:11*), He often times chooses to use others to provide for us so that not only are we being blessed, but they are as well. In *John 21:15-17* Jesus asks Simon (Peter) three times, "Do you love Me?" To which Simon replied, "Yes Lord, you know that I do." Then Jesus instructed Simon to tend to and feed His sheep.

In essence Jesus is saying if you love Me, help Me take care of My other sheep. This may mean to give them food, pay a bill, be there when they endure a trial, be a mentor, or any number of other ways. It takes a great deal of strength to extend comfort and support in person to those hurting or struggling. In turn, you are being "Jesus" to them. Jesus never shies away from anyone. He always meets them where they are, whether in grief, sorrow, or sin, and He extends comfort, support, and a way out of their situation—through salvation.

When we tend and feed His sheep, our blessings come in the form of personal comfort, renewed strength, and a peace of realizing that our presence, our show of love toward them, brought them peace. Furthermore, when we realized that God Himself went with us and provided our strength, love, peace, and so forth, our assurance is elevated that God truly loves us and has fulfilled His guarantee, which is written throughout the Bible as "God with us." You see, when we take God with us everywhere we go, we then have opportunities to leave Him everywhere we go. In turn, when we truly feed His sheep, when we go when and where God sends us, God is able to extend His promises of salvation, strength, peace, patience, love, goodness and so forth to all with whom we come in contact. Then they have the same opportunity to receive His offerings.

God's offerings are available to all at all times, as Jesus states in *Luke 11:9-10, "And I say unto you, Ask, and it shall be given you; seek, and ye shall find; knock, and it shall be opened unto you. For every one that asketh receiveth; and he that seeketh findeth; and to him that knocketh it shall be opened." (KJV)*

Chris and I not only asked—we begged! Neither of us slept the night Faith met Jesus. We were so tormented and broken that we laid awake the entire night begging God to "Help us!" We prayed for ourselves, and we prayed for each other through tears and the deepest anguish we had ever known. God heard our prayers, and He answered our prayers with the strength to **live** through the night and then the strength to meet the next morning.

God provided for my needs that Friday morning when He placed my pastor and youth minister in my yard. Saturday morning He again provided what Chris and I both needed through family and friends.

Earlier Saturday morning before everyone arrived, after crying together more, and after Kristen had awakened. Chris went to the bed room to dress. He then frantically called for me to come there. As soon as he did, I knew what he had found.

I walked into the bedroom to find Chris standing beside our bed looking at the rail. He said to me, "Look, Faith wrote her name on our bed."

At that very moment God spoke to me and I told Chris, "No, God is telling us to keep the "**Faith**."

I began to explain that I had seen her name on our bed Friday morning after I had gotten her back into the bed when she had thrown up that one last time. I did not say anything to her because I knew that she felt bad and I realized that at some point she felt like getting out of bed to write her name.

Chris realized at that moment that as he lay crying out to God all night and considering suicide, where Faith had written her name was the very spot where he tightly held keeping himself from getting out of bed to kill himself.

Not only was "Faith" written on our bed, but it was written outward so that we could read it as we walked up to the bed. So Faith did not write it lying down. God gave her the strength to get out of bed and write her name to remind us that He is there and that He is in control.

Again God used Faith to give us what we needed at that moment, just as He had used her to give us what we needed when she was just four years old and asked me if I was going to have another baby. For now my strength also came from the knowledge that we had to raise Kristen. Not just to adulthood, but to Love and accept Christ just as Faith had done with her whole life.

God offers much to us. God offers all He has to us at all times. Just as we have a choice to follow Christ or to follow Satan, we also have a choice to accept God's offerings. If we do not accept them, we will be left in a crippled state of being.

"Blessed be God, even the Father of our Lord Jesus Christ, the Father of mercies, and the God of all comfort; Who comforteth us in all our tribulation, that we may be able to comfort them which are in any trouble, by the comfort wherewith we ourselves are comforted of God. For as the sufferings of Christ abound in us, so our consolation also aboundeth by Christ. And whether we be afflicted, it is for your consolation and salvation, which is effectual in the enduring of the same sufferings which we also suffer:

or whether we be comforted, it is for your consolation and salvation," 2 Corinthians 1:3-6 (KJV).

God wants us to choose His offerings of comfort, love, peace, strength, joy, patience, and so forth, so that He can reward us with His ultimate gift of eternal life; *"For the wages of sin is death; but the gift of God is eternal life through Jesus Christ our Lord,"* Romans 6:23 (KJV).

Faith loves Jesus with all her heart and soul. I have no doubts that she is with the Father, Son, and Holy Spirit in heaven alive and well with her sister Katherine and her twin sibling that we were never blessed to see. Faith accepted God's offerings as a child, and she has received her crown of life in the presence of our Lord.

Furthermore, when our lives on earth are complete, we will instantly be reunited with our children forever in heaven in the presence of our Lord. *("We are confident, I say, and willing rather to be absent from the body, and to be present with the Lord,"* 2 Corinthians 5:8, KJV).

Dear friend, consider choosing God right now to receive Jesus and all His wonderful offerings along with the opportunity to meet our beautiful young soldiers of Christ: Faith, her twin sibling, and Katherine at the end of your time in this world. (*"Whereas ye know not what shall be on the morrow. For what is your life? It is even a vapour, that appeareth for a little time, and then vanisheth away,"* James 4:1, KJV). It only takes a prayer; a discussion with God. "Father, I love you and want to follow Christ the rest of my life. Father, please send Jesus to enter my heart, and to control my life according to Your desires, and to fill my life with Your abundance and Joy. Amen."

Dear brother or sister, when your vapor has vanished from this earth, where will it flow next; in the glorious presence of our Lord God in heaven, or in the treacherous presence of Satan and his demons in hell?

Chapter 4

Healing: Going Back In Order To Move Ahead

*"The Spirit of the Lord is upon Me, because He hath anointed Me to preach the gospel to the poor; **He hath sent Me to heal the brokenhearted**, to preach deliverance to the captives, and recovering of sight to the blind, to set at liberty them that are bruised."*
Luke 4:18 (KJV)

Indeed my heart is broken in many, many pieces. I still have days (and know that I always will) that as soon as I open my eyes, I cry all day and will not be able to function well at all. There is absolutely no forgetting a loved one who has passed on, especially when that loved one is your child. The sorrow is forever there, and each day I carry a heart with a void the size of a mountain.

I spent eight years loving and living with Faith, watching her grow into a beautiful, sweet young girl. I spent seven months loving and living with Katherine, watching her grow into a beautiful, sweet young baby. I spent only days loving our miscarried twin baby, who I did not even know existed until he or she was gone. Now I live with the despair of never having the opportunity to see him or her in any form, and never watching Faith and Katherine grow to adulthood. I will, however, spend the rest of my life in love with God our Father. He loved me enough to sacrifice His son Jesus long ago for all my children to live today. Although they are not with me here on earth, they are with Him in heaven—a place called paradise (*Luke 23:43*).

Just as a portion of *Luke 4:18* states, God sent Jesus to heal the brokenhearted. As Jesus is one part of the Trinity, He is one part of the whole, therefore being God, God himself came back to earth as baby Jesus to heal His children's disbeliefs and turn them back to believing in Him. If we, the brokenhearted, would accept His offering of healing, He will lead us back to life, and to one that is more abundant than before (*John 10:10*).

Chris and I will spend the rest of our earthly lives brokenhearted. We carry a void in our hearts that is absolutely unknown to others, and completely unexplainable by us. This is remarkably true for every parent who has said "good-bye" to their child or children. Each parent loves their children in a distinctive way. Our children are a gift from God (*Psalm 127:3*) created through a love that He used to bring their parents together. These parents did not even know one another during the first portion of their lives. Then God allowed a chance meeting of two people who unbeknownst to them, will spend hopefully the rest of their lives together.

Therefore, just as the love between a man and a women who become parents is distinctive to them, the love they hold for their child is unmatched by others. The same can be said of grief. The grieving process also is a very personal process which is not shared by any two people, not even a husband and wife.

There were many times that I could not understand Chris's method of reasoning or grieving. Just as I am sure he felt the same for me during my grieving process. For example, Chris had to talk. In the days that followed Katherine and Faith's passing, Chris repeated the events that took place to anyone and everyone. This was just his way of dealing with the pain he experienced and his way of letting it out so as not to be consumed with sorrow and anger. During that same time, I was quiet. I barely spoke a word to anyone. I did not want to speak a word to anyone. I did not want to hear myself say the things that had taken place. Also, I was silently talking with God; praying without ceasing. I was holding everything in and letting God deal with me and with what I was feeling. As I look back to those days, I remember being aggravated with Chris for talking so much, all the while being very much thankful that he was doing the talking.

Chris and I shared one distinct feeling in Faith's death; that we had been robbed. Very much so we had been robbed. Faith was a beautiful, healthy eight-year-old girl who completely loved life. She thoroughly loved Christ and she loved going to church and participating in the many opportunities for children through Sunday school, Girls in Action, Choir, and AWANA. Additionally, she loved to go to the beach, to play soccer, and to play with her pets (5 dogs, 1 cat, and 1 rabbit). Faith asked me many times about being able to play soccer as an adult;

and, as I would tell her about the Olympic team just for women, her whole being exploded with excitement.

Faith's biggest worldly love was animals. She would watch every animal show on television. She would sit by our front window and draw the different birds that would land on the feeder just outside. She had many books on all different kinds of animals and would read them over and over.

Just before Faith turned seven she came to me one day and asked could she have another rabbit. Not wanting to break her heart, I told her that she would have to pray about the rabbit and ask God. Faith accepted that answer with a smile and ran back outside to play more with her dogs. Within ten minutes, Faith ran back into the house and screamed, "Mama, look what I got!" I could not believe my eyes. Faith was holding a wild baby bunny.

Faith with Wild Bunny

The dogs had disturbed their nest and chased the family of bunnies off in different directions. One of the baby bunnies had run right to one of her dogs and stopped at its feet. Faith then ran over to it and grabbed it before the dog could. Needless to say, there was no way I could tell her that she could not keep her gift from God.

We have truly been robbed. Not by God, but by Satan. Satan brought death and destruction into this world when he deceived Adam and Eve in the Garden of Eden. God explicitly told them not to eat of the tree of the Knowledge of Good and Evil, and if they did eat of this tree, they would surely die. Satan told Eve that they would not die, but have the same knowledge that God had.

As a result of their disobedience, they were cast out of the Garden of Eden, where the Tree of Life also lived. This was one of the many trees they could have eaten from. However, being cast out of the Garden, they no longer had access to this tree and death surely came to them just as God personally instructed them both (*Genesis 2:16-17*).

Today, Jesus is our "Tree of Life." The only action needed by people to gain everlasting life is to **believe in Jesus** (*John 3:16*). We do not have to physically eat of any fruit, we just have to believe in Jesus and feed on God's Word.

Chris and I know that Faith's birth was an answer to prayer, and that during the time of bleeding when her twin was miscarried, Faith was allowed to live when she too was probably supposed to have miscarried. Chris and I believe that God changed His mind as a result of prayer and allowed Faith to live—even though just eight years.

Oh what joy we have in her memory, all the pictures that beautify our modest home, and the knowledge that we will just be **separated** for a short time. We will be reunited when God calls us to heaven; a place called paradise. (*"Precious in the sight of the Lord, is the death of His saints,"* Psalm 116:15, NKJV).

Chris and I were married in February; and, when our anniversary rolled around in just two months after Faith's passing, Chris suggested that we take a short vacation. My first thoughts were GREAT! I really wanted (needed) a change of scenery and thought that getting away would be good for all of us.

Chris then said, "Let's go to the beach." My heart briefly stopped along with my breathing. I could not answer him because I knew with the way that he said it that he really wanted to go to the beach. I did not. Faith loved the beach and she had taught me to love the beach. We went to the beach every summer with her. I could still see her playing in the surf acting like a little puppy running on all fours in and out of the water. The last thing I wanted was to go to the beach. Reluctantly I said, "Okay."

Chris chose to visit Tybee Island and since we had never gone there before, I felt better about the trip. Packing for the trip was much harder than I expected. Not packing Faith's things for the trip broke my heart all over again. I really wanted to just stay at home and never go anywhere again. It was too hard. The void in my heart felt like a ton of bricks lying on my chest. Breathing, speaking, and thinking were all difficult. With God's help, we were finally in the truck and headed out.

As Kristen slept, Chris and I had an opportunity to talk. Along with the sharing were tears as well. I used all my might to keep from completely breaking down and managed to just cry a little.

While stopping for lunch on the way, it was really nice to have the waitress look at us with a smile on her face and speak to us with a normal, joyful tone, even though she was just taking our order. We had not had that type of pleasantry in two months now—understandably so. That waitress may never know it, but she was "Jesus" to me that day.

When she smiled at us and spoke to us joyfully, I was then able to return the favor. It felt good to smile again and to also look into someone's eyes without having sorrow looking back (*"To give light to them that sit in darkness and in the shadow of death, to guide our feet into the way of peace," Luke 1:79, KJV*).

God had led me there. As badly as I did not want to go, He guided me to that way of peace. God knew that for me to move ahead, I had to go back to what was normal for me and my family. I had to smile again and react with people in a happy, joyful manner. He knew that I was not going to experience that attribute at home with friends and family for they were also broken. He took me to a stranger (an angel) in a restaurant to begin my healing.

At the hotel my soul began to stir again. Walking into our room I could smell the beach, hear the waves crashing, and the seagulls calling. The tears were harder and harder to hold back as floods of memories poured into my mind. I could see Faith bouncing around every hotel we had ever visited, wide-eyed with the excitement of being somewhere new and the opportunity to splash in the ocean.

It was that moment when I thought I would fall apart. I felt the tears welling, and my heart began to race to the point of being so agitated that I could not sit still. All I could think about was walking out to that beach. I just knew my world would crash all around me and that my strength would disappear. I just knew that I would be broken to incredible sobbing, and I was afraid that I could not, would not be able to stop.

The first step onto the sand of that beach was incredibly difficult. My emotions grew to a level of pressure that had my speech interrupted, my eyes welling with tears, and my body tense and rigid. I did not believe that I could walk any length of the beach that day; or any other day.

Just as I was feeling the pressure mounting and on the verge of crying uncontrollably, Kristen took off running and laughing as she gleefully chased the seagulls trying with all her might to catch one. Before I knew it, I was smiling as I watched her joyfully bounce across the sand smiling from ear to ear; once again full of life.

Kristen Ann

Isaiah 40:29 states, *"He giveth power to the faint; and to them that have no might he increaseth strength." (KJV).* God gave me power and strength at that very moment on the beach when He moved my thoughts from "what I had" to "what I have."

I was allowing my circumstance to control my life by fixating on what I had lost instead of praising God for what He had given me. Not only had He allowed us to have Faith for eight wonderful years, He allowed us to witness her ask Christ into her heart, to be astonished when she publicly professed her faith by walking the church isle alone and then to see her baptized and know in our hearts that she was saved. He also gave us Kristen—our beautiful little red-headed ball of fire.

God our Father knew that we would need strength beyond measure when He had to call Faith home, and He delivered that very strength through Kristen. There I was on that beach realizing that I could smile again; that I could feel joy again; that I could live again. (*"The thief does not come except to steal, and to kill, and to destroy. I have come that they may have life, and that they may have it more abundantly," John 10:10, NKJV*). By trusting in God and keeping my eyes on Jesus' example, my life slowly and assuredly began again.

It was still difficult to enjoy the beach to the fullest that day. I found myself crying a little every time Chris and Kristen got out of my sight. I know for sure that I needed those times of mourning in order to believe all of God's promises of heaven and instead of saying "good-bye" to Faith while walking on that beach, Jesus helped me to see that I needed only to say her, "See you soon".

Jesus made this very clear in *Matthew 19:14 (NKJV)* when He said to the disciples, *"Let the little children come to Me, and do not forbid them; for of such is the kingdom of Heaven."* Jesus plainly says that children have a place in Heaven, just as the adults. Not only is heaven one of His many promises, but in *2 Corinthians 5:8* Paul writes, *"We are confident, yes, well pleased rather to be absent from the body and to be present with the Lord." (NKJV)* Therefore we can be confident in knowing that our loved ones who have passed from this world have passed to the presence of the Lord—Paradise!

Dear friend, Jesus carried me back to the beach in order for me to go forth and live—for Him. Many times throughout that following year, I had to go back in order to move ahead. I had to go back to the various activities of the church that I had enjoyed with Faith for eight years. I had to go back to our favorite restaurants, back to the library, back to the park, back to the grocery store, back to the leisurely walks through the woods, and back to the swimming pool. I even found myself going back to her elementary school. I had to go back to living in order to make a life for Chris and Kristen, and in order to continue living for Christ.

I can boldly claim *Psalm 13:5-6* right along with King David who wrote this particular passage that, *"But I have trusted in Your mercy; My heart shall rejoice in Your salvation. ⁶ I will sing to the LORD, Because He has dealt bountifully with me." (NKJV)*

God has truly dealt bountifully with me. Not only did He lead me back to life after allowing three vital parts of my life to be taken away, but He was right there with me leading the way, and carrying me when I could not stand on my own two feet. It takes trusting our Lord with all our heart and understanding (knowing) that He knows what is best for His children. *"Trust in the LORD with all your heart, And lean not on your own understanding; In all your ways acknowledge Him, And He shall direct your paths. Do not be wise in your own eyes; Fear the LORD and depart from evil.* **It will be health to your flesh, And strength to your bones,***" Proverbs 3:5-8 (NKJV).*

Chapter 5

Trusting Our Father

"Therefore I will look unto the LORD; I will wait for the God of my salvation: my God will hear me. Rejoice not against me, O mine enemy: when I fall, I shall arise; when I sit in darkness, the LORD shall be a light unto me." Micah 7:7-8 (KJV)

For me to move ahead was just as hard as going back to life. At the time Faith died, I was greatly involved in ministry within our church, as well as the community through the CMC ministry. The hardest activity for me to return to was being "Commander" of the AWANA ministry for children three-years-old through sixth grade. This is where I had to look unto the Lord and **TRUST** that He would fulfill my strength.

AWANA is a ministry where children spend two hours having Bible study, reciting memorized Scripture, and enjoying a game time. AWANA is the acronym for "Approved Workmen Are Not Ashamed" and is based on the Scripture from *2 Timothy 2:15, which is "Study to shew thyself approved unto God, a workman that needeth not to be ashamed, rightly dividing the word of truth." (KJV)*

In 2005 I had been asked to serve as the Commander (a fancy name for overall director) for this ministry since I had been involved in working with the children for five years; the start of the program at our church. So here I was managing this magnificent program for the first time. I had spent the past five years teaching Faith's age group that God was with those who believe in Him all the time and that He would get them through anything they could possibly face on this earth.

All those years, of course, I was secretly speaking of God my Father carrying me through the death of our baby, Katherine, and how He was right there with me and my family the entire time carrying us when we needed carrying and strengthening us to move ahead when we needed strengthening. I did not realize that I was about to be tested in the worst way.

When Faith died on December 9, AWANA was in the middle of a break for the Thanksgiving and Christmas holidays. This break allowed our adult and children's choirs their opportunity for rehearsal and decorating the gym for the annual musicals. However, AWANA had not yet celebrated Christmas, and I had planned our party for the week after Christmas, while the children would still be enjoying their school break. So here I was, the Commander, in need of planning the children's Christmas party; our eight-year-old-daughter, who loved this program, had died two weeks before Christmas.

"Therefore I will look unto the LORD; I will wait for the God of my salvation: my God will hear me," Micah 7:7 (KJV). This was one time I not only had to look to the Lord, but had to desperately cry out for help, and trust that He would hear and answer.

Even with a solid foundation in Christ and having full knowledge that Faith is alive and well in Heaven, when she entered her eternal life, we were left with a life of separation anxiety, and were drawn to church more than ever. We went every time the doors opened. With each message through our pastor and Sunday school teachers, God spoke straight to us with words of courage, strength, life, and love. We continued to trust God through all that we were experiencing and knew that we had to "look unto the Lord" at all times.

I had been thrown into the largest spiritual warfare so far, and Satan was standing ready to use any avenue offered to creep into my life and destroy what God had created. This Christmas party could have been an avenue. However, I chose to cast my cares upon Jesus (*1 Peter 5:7*), and let Him work through the details.

Hebrews 2:14-18 says, *"Forasmuch then as the children are partakers of flesh and blood, he also himself likewise took part of the same; that through death he might destroy him that had the power of death, that is, the devil; And deliver them who through fear of death were all their lifetime subject to bondage. For verily he took not on him the nature of angels; but he took on him the seed of Abraham. Wherefore in all things it behoved him to be made like unto his brethren, that he might be a merciful and faithful high priest in things pertaining to God, to make reconciliation for the sins of the people. For in that he himself hath suffered being tempted, he is able to succour them that are tempted." (KJV)*

God reminds us that Jesus experienced this life the same, exact way that we are experiencing it now. Therefore, He understands fully all our circumstances; especially the pain and sorrow. With Jesus's death comes Jesus's resurrection; which destroyed the power of death.

Let us take a moment to understand "the power of death" as mentioned here. Death leaves the living broken and sorrowful. To the living, death means that someone has stopped existing; never again to hear their voice, see their smile, feel their touch, or even enjoy their fragrance. Death leaves the living in a continuous burdened state of missing someone who cannot be visited.

A loved one's death controls one's thoughts, actions, emotions—our very being. Death changes the person we once were. Jesus's death destroyed the power of death, releasing those who fear death as being an end, by being the beginning of life eternal; never ending.

Jesus told the disciples in *John 14:2-3* that His Father's house has many mansions where He himself was going to prepare a place for you. Better still Jesus says in verse three that He will come again and receive you to Himself, and that where He is, you may be also.

Within these two verses, Jesus is explaining that His earthly body is going to be destroyed by the sin of this world, through Satan having control over people of this world, but that He was going to live in His Father's house, and while He's there He's going to be busy preparing your place and awaiting His time to come and get you to live out eternity where He is—Hallelujah!

God instructed the anonymous author of *Psalm 116:15* to put this guarantee into a perspective we would find comfort in, and He states, *"Precious in the sight of the LORD is the death of His saints." (KJV)* God finds the death of His saints (believers and followers) precious, because we then get to join Him in Heaven for all eternity in a glorified existence.

Furthermore, the remaining Hebrews 2:14-18 passage explains that Jesus had to be made like His brethren, which is all believers, so that He would be God's merciful and faithful High Priest to us. Therefore, Jesus's life and death prepared Him to understand the sufferings of this world, in order for Him to perfectly aid you and me through our temptations and trials.

Yes, dear one, Satan will use the death of our loved ones as a temptation to draw our focus from Christ our Savior, our true Brother. Remember, *Hebrews 2:14-17* states that Jesus is our merciful and "faithful" High Priest. If we remain faithful to Him through trusting Him always, He will be faithful to us by always providing our deepest needs every step of the way.

As the children's Christmas party began with setting-up inflatable jumpers and putting out food, those helping me continued to say, "I don't know how you do it."

One person even asked, "Do you ever cry?"

At that moment, I realized just how well Christ was faithful in sustaining me through brokenness. Inside I was completely in ruin. I hated to look directly into anyone's eyes because they then would see the raised, red veins, and notice the large bags underneath my own eyes. They would realize that I was spending most of my time crying and hardly any time sleeping. So the question of do I cry not only shocked me, it also made me know how God was fulfilling His guarantee of strength through weakness (*2 Corinthians 12:9*). It was then that I knew I would get through this party.

As the children arrived, some of them came and hugged me with their beautiful eyes welling with tears, unable to speak a word. Then God whispered a question in my ear, "Are you going to be the example of what you've been teaching them for five years?"

I knew the answer was "Yes."

Many years before I had taken *Philippians 4:13* as my life verse which states, *"I can do all things through Christ who strengthens me."* *(NKJV)* This was truly one of those things. To my surprise, I enjoyed those kids. I forced my thoughts to be of Christ. Knowing that Faith was alive and well in her mansion prepared by Christ Himself, and that He himself had come and received her to His presence in Paradise. The rest of the night those children and I laughed and joked just as we always had, and boy did it feel good to laugh again and enjoy a sampling of joyfulness in the midst of brokenness.

Faith's best friend Adeleigh Hamilton was there trying to have fun. Even though she played with the other kids, her beautiful, innocent face described her broken, shock-riddled heart.

Adeleigh is a lovely 'social butterfly', never meeting a stranger and always wearing a large, beautiful smile. But, at this party, she was out of place. She and Faith had been inseparable at church; always together in class and at play.

Now, Adeleigh looked exactly how I felt. Her joy was gone. Her big, beautiful, brown eyes were now emotionless and sad. Her face was expressionless from shock. My heart broke all over again each time I looked into her eyes.

I secretly prayed for Adeleigh all through the party. I begged for God to bring her peace and, of course, a new best friend. I also felt guilty. She had befriended my child, and it was my child who had instantly gone away. I felt I had caused Adeleigh's pain.

As I prayed, God filled me with peace and helped me to understand that the guilt I was feeling was from Satan. This avenue opened for him and he quickly used it for his deed of pulling me away from Christ; away from life.

God reminded me that it was Satan who brought death and destruction into this, His, world and made it corruptible. Therefore, as I called out to God, He answered with more of His guarantees—God with us, peace, strength, and knock and it shall be opened unto you.

God filled both Adeleigh and me with His strength, which allowed us to enjoy celebrating His Son's birthday through play and laughter.

God enabled me to stand with Him as the very example to those children He sent me there to be. God is always with us and by trusting our Father, He will carry us through anything we could possibly face on this earth.

That night, I walked out of the party, once again in disbelief at the strength flowing through my being. I remembered the verse so appropriate for Christmas, as well as daily life for those who love God, *"Behold, a virgin shall be with child, and shall bring forth a son, and they shall call his name Emmanuel, which being interpreted is, God with us," Matthew 1:23 (KJV).*

God began my healing as I left the party. By trusting our Father, asking for His help, and receiving His guarantees, I was able to take part in a party that I really did not want to attend; not to mention plan and lead. However, God knew I needed to **TRUST** Him completely. He allowed me to enjoy that party (those kids) so that I could go back the following week as the leader and teacher to the very group Faith just left.

God says in *Jeremiah 33:3, "Call to Me, and I will answer you, and show you great and mighty things, which you do not know." (NKJV)* God is always waiting for us to ask for His help and direction. He is not pushy; He will not force himself into our lives. We have to go to Him. That is the only way God knows that we truly love Him, and that is the only way we will know that we truly love Him.

I now have an unshakeable, unmovable **TRUST** in God, because I know that He is with me, that He loves me, that He cares for me, and that He covers me in all that I now live with.

Paul, an apostle of Christ, said it best when he wrote *2 Timothy 1:7-12* which states:

"For God hath not given us the spirit of fear; but of power, and of love, and of a sound mind. Be not thou therefore ashamed of the testimony of our Lord, nor of me his prisoner: but be thou partaker of the afflictions of the gospel according to the power of God; Who hath saved us, and called us with an holy calling, not according to our works, but according to his own purpose and grace, which was given us in Christ Jesus before the world began, But is now made manifest by the appearing of our Saviour Jesus Christ, who hath abolished death, and hath brought life and immortality to light through the gospel: Whereunto I am appointed a preacher, and an apostle, and a teacher of the Gentiles. For the which cause I also suffer these things: nevertheless I am not ashamed: for I know whom I have believed, and am persuaded that he is able to keep that which I have committed unto him against that day." (KJV)

Only God can show you the mighty things of this earth that pertain to you as He is the one who created this earth and gave you life. If you ask Him daily as 'The Lord's Prayer' (*Matthew 6:9-13 and Luke 11:1-4*) directs, God will lead you through the horrors of this world and instill a peace beyond understanding (*Philippians 4:7*); of which is understanding and knowing that we are not to live for this life on earth, but that this life on earth is preparation for our eternal life with the Trinity (Father, Son, and Holy Spirit).

Therefore, to have the abundant life Jesus speaks of in *John 10:10*, especially after tragedy, one must **TRUST** Jesus. You must allow Him to work by taking the hard steps of returning to the life you had before the tragedy. When you do, you will see God at work as He provides the strength, peace, and guidance to take back your life.

As your **TRUST** grows through this process, so will your **JOY** and then will you receive your abundant life. This process has worked for me and countless others, it is proven, and it will work for you.

God's very own Adam and Eve experienced the death of one of their children, Abel. To make this pain strikingly deeper, Abel died at the hand of his brother Cain. The torment Adam and Eve must have lived with, I just cannot imagine. Their trust in God allowed them to continue their lives as the Bible explains that they moved ahead with life and had more children.

God's guarantees helped reestablish Adam and Eve, many others listed in God's Word, countless others who have experienced their child's death in this world, and God will, if you allow, reestablish you with a joyful life of abundance.

Chapter 6

Living Joyfully Again

"Blessed be God, even the Father of our Lord Jesus Christ, the Father of mercies, and the God of all comfort; Who comforteth us in all our tribulation, that we may be able to comfort them which are in any trouble, by the comfort wherewith we ourselves are comforted of God." 2 Corinthians 1:3-4, KJV.

As each month passed throughout that first year without Faith, our strength grew along with our grace. By trusting in God's guarantees, and receiving His offerings we are, I am, living again.

We know that our grieving will end only when we greet our children at heaven's golden gates. For now, we must concentrate on living this life, but not for ourselves, for our Father God, His Son Jesus our Savior, and His helper the Holy Spirit indwelling within us.

Had Jesus not come to this earth as a baby and grown to a man experiencing this world the same way we do, we would not have His perfect example. As Christ was completely God when he lived here on earth, He also was completely human. Therefore, Jesus lived fully as we do now, and Jesus understands everything we will experience (*Hebrews 2:14-16*).

I quickly realized that I (we) had only been separated from Faith, Katherine, and our unborn child for a moment in time. God tells us that we are just a vapor ourselves (*James 4:14*), which will be gone from this earth at a moment's notice. Even though it feels like I will live another life-time before being reunited with my children, when I arrive in heaven, the trip will be sudden—in the twinkling of an eye (*1 Corinthians 15:52*).

Therefore everyone should live each day with their "essential" affairs in order; by which I mean your "love affair" with God, Jesus, and the

Holy Spirit. These are the only affairs that will matter to you when your vapor has vanished.

I can assure you that if your affairs with the Trinity are in order; all your earthly affairs will automatically be in place (*Matthew 5:48*). You will then receive your crown of life (*Revelations 2:10*), your very own mansion (*John 14:1-2*) prepared especially for you by Jesus Christ Himself, and you will be reunited with your loved ones.

Additionally, I realized that God Himself experienced my very pain. As I considered Jesus: who always was, always is, and always will be. I came to understand that He had to leave heaven (the presence of His Father-God) and enter earth as a baby, and then grow into a man to give us the one true example to follow (*Hebrews 4:14-15*). For 33 years God separated Himself from Jesus (His Son) for my (your) sake.

God sat on His thrown in heaven and watched His beloved Son experience love, happiness, compassion, rejection, shame, and physical pain for others and from others while preparing a way for us. Oh how God's heart must have been repeatedly torn out, ripped apart, and broken to pieces—at our ignorance, sinfulness, and disobedience.

However, God knew that with Their suffering, Jesus was developing into the Light of the World, which will illuminate clearly our paths to God, and will be able to carry us through our suffering by following Jesus's perfect example of calling out to God in everything (*"Pray without ceasing," 1 Thessalonians 5:17*). Jesus is the perfect testimony for God, His love for us, and His power over this world.

Because of Jesus's trials and triumph over Satan, I am able to live again and so can you. Jesus said, *"I have come that they may have life, and that they may have it more abundantly," John 10:10b (NKJV)*, so I urge you to follow Jesus to a more abundant life than before your tragedy, by accepting all that He has to freely offer. There is no charge, we only have to believe in Jesus, and that He will give us what we need, when we need it. Then we will receive His gifts and live a life of abundance.

Throughout this book you have read, and hopefully understand, that it takes trusting in God to live this earthly life. You must allow Him to love you in order to receive His comforts of knowledge, which brings peace, strength, and yes joy.

Psalms 118:13 and 14 states, "You pushed me violently that I might fall: but the LORD helped me. The LORD is my strength and song, and is become my salvation." (NKJV) The death of our children is definitely the act of Satan pushing us violently. It is his brutal attempt to push us away from God. Satan's only desire in this world is to cause people to disbelieve God and to follow his destructive path.

We have to trust God by calling to Him for His help of comfort. When we continue to seek God through hardship and trials, He strengthens us to endure that turbulent time of this life. He allows us to see that it is, in fact, God at work supporting us. This permits us to sing out a testimony that we know God to be true, because we have first-hand knowledge. God saves us from Satan's wrath by drawing near and strengthening our relationship with Him, and at the same time Satan will be dispelled from our presence and us from Satan's impending doom as stated in *James 4:7-8, "Therefore submit to God. Resist the devil and he will flee from you. Draw near to God and He will draw near to you. Cleanse your hands, you sinners; and purify your hearts, you double-minded." (NKJV)*

Once this has happened, we have an obligation to God, which is found in *Hebrews 4:16*; and says, *"Let us therefore come boldly to the throne of grace, that we may obtain mercy and find grace to help in time of need." (NKJV)*

God is telling us here that Christ suffered this world for each one of us. He knows our suffering intimately and perfectly. Therefore, He is the Master who knows how to survive and how to show us that we can come to him at any time, with any burden, to find out exactly how to manage whatever it is troubling us. Then we will know definitely how to help someone else in their time of need (*2 Corinthians 1:4*).

In other words, He is telling us to testify on His behalf. Tell others what and how God has carried you through suffering. By doing so, you are being a witness for God unashamed. You are giving others an opportunity to have our Father as their Father, and thus, they will receive an abundant life here on earth and inherit similar precious rewards in heaven.

Having gone through tragedy, we become knowledgeable of tribulation. We understand its effects on our lives with its pain and emotional disarray. We understand what it is like to have our lives changed in an instant, without prior preparation.

If we have chosen to trust God and allow Him to restore our lives to an unexpected abundance, then we also understand the steps of faith needed to patiently wait for God to act in our lives on our behalf. With this knowledge we now have the understanding and preparation to help others experiencing a similar tragedy.

We know that there are no **words** that anyone could say to you that really help. *Second Corinthians 1:3-4* reminds us that God first comforts us in our tribulation so that we may be able to receive comfort from family and friends, and to then be able to comfort others at another time. God's Word tells us that He and Christ know full well the exact pain we are suffering; therefore, they are qualified to comfort you and me.

Of all the people who reached out to me at both my children's deaths, the people who comforted me most were the ones who had already experienced a similar tragedy. Their demeanor was humble in my presence, their words were humble when speaking, and their eyes carried a vision of sorrow that I understood and to which I could relate. Therefore, I know God had sent them to me for they were emulating Christ's compassion.

I fully believe that those particular brothers and sisters had also followed Christ's instruction from *Hebrews 4:16* in that before coming to my aid, they went boldly to the throne of grace and obtained the mercy and grace to comfort me in my time of need.

What this means is that each one of them prayed (talked) to God openly and shared their love and compassion for me, to which God replied by giving them the strength to visit me (and my family) with the appropriate mercy and grace needed to keep my focus on our Father.

Now, I have been prepared to comfort others with the very same comfort God has bestowed in me. I truly have a heart for people. Not necessarily for only those who have experienced, or will experience, any tribulation, but for all people to have the knowledge of God, Jesus, and the Holy Spirit. The Trinity is in place for your good, not your demise. It does not matter who you are, or who you used to be. What matters is that you accept the truth of what you have heard, believing and knowing in your heart that you are loved by God.

All that He has done for my family and me, He will do that and more for you. Jesus stands at the door knocking. He desperately wants you to open the door of your heart and mind and welcome Him in! When you open that door and allow Him to come in, you will be allowed to sit with Him on His throne, as Jesus sat with His Father on His throne; *"Behold, I stand at the door and knock. If anyone hears My voice and opens the door, I will come in to him and dine with him, and he with Me. To him who overcomes I will grant to sit with Me on My throne, as I also overcame and sat down with My Father on His throne. He who has an ear, let him hear what the Spirit says to the churches," Revelations 3:20-22 (NKJV).*

For more information,
please contact Shirley at:

96 Indian Ridge Drive
North Augusta, SC 29860
(803) 442-3728
www.sharing-his-bread.com
mcbride62367@netzero.com